SHAKE-
SPEARE'S
DOG

THE BIRTHPLACE

SHAKE-SPEARE'S DOG

a novel by Leon Rooke

ALFRED A.
KNOPF
NEW
YORK
1983

For Gordon Lish

I am indebted to Professor Edward Berry of the University of Victoria for his invaluable counsel in matters of historical accuracy.

L. R.

SHAKE-SPEARE'S
DOG

1

꩜ ꩜ ꩜ That spongy, water-licking Wolfsleach was down on the grass doing sport with Marr, and when he saw me romping toward him with choppers flaring, he whirled in gummy panic and gave Marr a great kick in her hind parts that sent her spinning over on all fours, whimpering her sorrows at pleasure abated and leaking drool from her yellow mouth. Agh, you wench, I thought, you thrush-throated, humping dog; oh, the Devil take you. So I tagged her one on the fly, a quick bite that tozed gristle and fur, and kept on going. Blech and blah, woof and roar—oh, you mangy huffers with pig's feet for brains, here humping away to heart's content—and in *my* yard! There goes dignity, as the barrel-eyed Two Foots would say. Well, you'll taste the poison of my fangs, you'll get Hooker's come-upperance and what-for. You'll have *my* claw studs where dogger was. Woof-woof and arf-arf, damn you all.

Wolfsleach was up and running, the slake, but as he had no place to go except from wall to wall and around one leafless elm, I soon had the dribbler dough-footed in my punches, with his tail between his legs and crying like a headless mummer, "Don't hit me, Mr. Hooker, I was only— I was doing nothing wrong!" So I raked him again, the sly rudesby, for lying as much as for dickering poor Marr, whose addled spirit had picked up now to the extent that she was chasing us from wall to wall and around the stunted elm, nipping indiscriminately at our heels and tripping me up as I sought to corner Wolfs-leach and dip my chops thirty times into his bushy face.

Agh and etch (blech and blah), you piddler, you leaf-sniffing pooch!

I had been searching for the cur all morning long, since the minute I'd noticed he'd pizzled my bloodmate Terry and made her bloom.

"I'm sorry, Mr. Hooker," the potato-head whined. "Don't you go believing all you see. No, I wouldn't do nothing wrong either to your sister Terry or to your love's breath Marr, from whom I was only juicing fleas."

"Aye," I said, "and here's fleas for you, nasty hedge-hog, thou jouncing hen's dung and bawdy-basket. I'll soon have your bones dusted and ready for the charnel house." And I hit him again, this time from one side to the other of his gorbellied flanks and on his noodle, and with rich venom quaking fullway down my spine, I kept on throttling and maiming the sodden piece.

"Call yourself a dog?" I spat out. "Agh, you will stay swinish in your ways for all I preach, and I'm up to my gizzard's rear end with the lot of you. Foam at one end or the other, that's all you tail-waggers know, damn your cawkered hides!"

"Nay, whoa," the shitter groaned. "I'm whipped, Mr. Hooker. I've dawned on to the error of my ways. I'm set right to learning now."

But I'd heard all this before, e'en a thousand times,

and kept on laying full-sweat into the dismal slug. In truth, I was in my cock-walking mood, as for too long I had let principle slide, and in the absence of my tyranny, rough slacktimes had instilled the crow's breath over our yard. "Woof-woof, grr and growl," I said, "take this and that, demented beast, thou feast of a cesspool!" I wanted the bugger's blood between my teeth, to slurp up his guts and glory for my own mixed estate—to get my hot belly's full.

Marr, I noticed, was squat-tail down, rubbing her ort-hole against scratch grass, trying to erase some late gush-backing sting.

"Joy to itch in a minute," I heard her groan. "Oh, what profit in humping, anyway, when it always comes to this?"

And I wished I had tozed her harder, the no-dreaming, hog-shouldered, hog-stupored bitch.

Dog wants more, I thought, than this.

"Mercy, Mr. Hooker," the crapper Wolfsleach screeched, no doubt feeling the firmament's full ungodly woe had dumped down on him. I had my fangs locked on one ear, out to tear ear from his soggy brain, though in truth it was the whole of the boneless earth I yearned to rip asunder. Yea, that was my quest, to put it mildly. Somewhere between crust and core, I rigged, there must be something more chewy than a mutt's ear, something that could sweeten my dogly vinegar.

"Don't murder me, Mr. Hooker!"

"I'll give you murder, you scab. I'll skin your feathers inside out." And my fangs came down on his fat tongue, closed on his miserable, unlettered jaw. Squirt of blood, good. Another squirt, better yet. He let out a death gate's gleap of pain and rolled over, playing dead, giving his hind crutches a twitch. Yet I kept chomping. Ugg and awgg. Good. Meat of slackard dog.

It brought no rapture but put a flutter of hope to my dark mood. It did something to the putrid hum in my chest. My ceilings lifted a bit.

"Don't maim him, Mr. Hooker," Marr the cockroach begged.

Oh, the mean blindness of her: that she didn't know, could never see (or care at what she saw), that Wolf, herself, and every other dog came to their cribs already maimed. In their spirit, in their stringy brains. Maimed by falsehoods, their own deceits, by treachery of blood and power of tick, by the canon of Canutus and expeditation's knock-kneed curse—by man's inhumanity to dog. Black rage swirled inside me at these thoughts, flapping above my brows like a dozen vultures strung to a single wing, and for a moment blinding fury spun me flat. I wanted to stamp out the whole of dog, our entire half-trumped-up race, to put the blinkers on us all. Dog? To be dog? Then what's the use! I let loose of Wolf and flung myself at Marr, to rattle her in all her startled parts. I raked a claw straight down her face.

"You're crazed!" she flung out. "A wife-beater like that Two Foot you cleap to, the pimply Will!"

Lies now. What next from a cockroach dog?

She streaked behind Wolf, hoping for safer nest. Content to let that brute catch the brunt of my itching teeth. I romped into both of them. Paw and jaw, arf-arf, woof-woof. (Bow-wow.) I yanked hairs from their necks, sunk talon and heel into their eyes, dug hot licks into their chests. Wholehearted mayhem was all dogs of their league would ever understand. Like feeble swans, they

tried scratching away. But Hooker's lava poured after
them.

"Mercy, mercy—oh, someone save us!" the piddlers
cried.

Arf-arf, you shits! Bow-wow, you humping pugs!

Hooker, the whirlwind. Avenging dog.

We were making quite the whoobug when my master
Two Foot's kicksy-wicksy, the noxious Hathaway, still
stiff and pudged from laying eggs, howled in her drone's
eminence from the back door. I slowed down some,
thinking she might come with her cold water pots to
splash down on us, or with sticks hot as lightning bolts,
not to mention epithets so randomly obscene they'd cross
my eyes. But she was for the moment oblivious to dog,
her voice besotted with tender wooing, crafty appeal,
wifely caresses to soothe the swarthy air. Putting timid
inquiry to Will's shuttered scribbler's room above and
standing drab and pottled on her flat wide feet, as if the
whole of the world was to be shouldered by her wits
alone. By her hips' girth and tits' swell.

"There is no penny in the goose mug, my Will!" she
called.

"Oh, Willum, Susanna's got the chokes!"

"Oh, Will, my poke, your old Da is at his ale mum-
blings again!"

"Will? Will?"

But my Two Foot was master of her subterfuge and
wisely kept his visage clear. Acute with reason, warder's
law, he kept his throat muscles squelched.

"Oh, Mr. Shake, my peat!"

My peat, my pet, what a false snit this jailer was.

I could hear his deep-thought dropping down

draughts of fumy hebenon, juice of hemlock, thorny relish-of-pire, that her tongue-wag might be scalded shut and her curdled wifer's sauces be rat-licked away.

"Perish, hag!" I heard him say. But growled down through breeze that only canine could catch, for the calf had his natural fear of her. More than once she'd throttled him.

"Git thee a pitchfork and ride, ignominious witch."

"Will, your old mother needs buckets from the mere! Needs it now, my Will."

"Scat, Hathaway."

"And your honey needs her honey, sweet. One kiss? Open up, my saint."

Will stayed silent, the mouse.

She chunked a pebble or two at his shuttered sight-way, called twice and three times more. Then the dolorous wench heaved a resentful sigh, like a bog letting loose of vapors too long held. She struck up a snarly curse and finally went slug-footed back indoors.

My Two Foot's nose instantly snuckered forth.

"Has the drab biscuit gone?" he whispered to me. "The viper's got her sweetness," he growled to my nodding, "yet she's still the viper Hathaway. Let's boil the slut in oil."

I barked my feeling passion for his tune. But the scribbler's nose was already back at work.

The stooge. He'd been up there all day, minting rhyme, scratching dandruff from his empty head.

Words. How I hated them. (It ain't words, he'd say, but how they're shook.) As if words, his or mine, would ever have their day. Yet sight of the rogue made my humors lift. I could see some merit in the ghoulish English sky, in the clouds fermenting above us like a black gang of ticks . . .

And stood foolishly wagging tail, whining my degree of wanted fellowship up at him: Hooker awaits without, my liege. Let's for a man-and-dog walk along the Avon's shore or take fast tumble through Arden Wood. I'll give good ear to your mush and sprinkle on it a syllable or two of form.

My pause had given Wolfsleach the faint hope of slithering free. I lifted a claw from his belly further to encourage him in this view. And spat out his limp, salivered, half-devoured ear. Let the humper think what he wished. Let the scab think I was done with him. That Hooker's gorge was filled. Hope, even for a cur like him, is always there. I could feel under my pads his gross heart begin to swell. Let it, I thought. When he's idling in grass, ears laid back to snooze, I'll fry him in the true Hooker fat. I'll tear the sludge limb from limb.

Then, out of need mortifying to my self-image, I lifted leg and piddled over leaf and on head of some addled, brain-jerking bug and—dumb beast that I was— arightly and with arrogant aplomb loped off to lick my clack-dish. Oh, for supper! I thought. Oh, for a rack of bacon to confirm me on my do-gooder's path. Oh, for meated bone. Oh, for a carcass or two of whale.

Well, piss, I'd as soon pray to Sirius the Dogstar, for my clack-dish lacked even a smell. Not a tinge. Empty again. These Two Foots, including my wordy Shagsbier, couldn't be bothered with feeding dog. Better the dog should go on feeding them. My insides rumbled. Diet-of-Nothing's what I had. It had been three weeks since I'd had a bone between my paws, and that only one uprooted that had been chawed on a thousand times. Some knee's joint, some Pope's gristle, peasant's toe left over from the Middle Ages (on the whole, a friendlier period). Bleached by the mindless energy of a hundred gloppy years. ("Chew it pointy," Will had said. "I'll stab the witch with it as she sleeps.")

Dog wants more, I tell you. A field of hares, all boxed in, nowhere to run. To ride the backs of Sir Lucy's deers.

And more yet. Wants quitting of this corn-shucking town.

Marr was stretched out on the boards across the old tanning pit. Eyes at blinker on the world, or such, from her closed web, that she wished to see of it. I gave the harlot a shriveling stare. She took it with a pouty, maddening grin. "I don't like you," she glomped. "You've changed. You get more like the Two Foots every day."

Piddle on the cur.

Wolf limped over to lay his head down on her, whining like a bowlegged toad complaining how I'd broke his legs. To lift a hooded glance at me, saying, "Marr's right, Mr. Hooker. You've gone round the bend. You've turned against dog. Next, we know, you'll be wearing pants. You'll be scribbling too." Though he wouldn't say it out loud. But it would be what he'd go drumming into another dog's ear: "Pzzzzt. . . . Hooker thinks he's Two Foot. . . . Watch out for Hooker."

Piddle piddle. I'd as soon be lowing cow for all the change in dog I wrought.

My scop's mother, old Mary, came out and beat a rag against the steps. Then flopped it over her shoulders, said, "Don't I look pretty? Don't you dogs have nothing to do?" and stomped back inside, weary as a load of coal.

A rat came up from the bowels of the house and gnawed down to glom on whatever it was he thought he saw. A spot of blood bedizened his chin, and I wondered what it was he'd found to be chewing on. Another rat was my guess. Or maybe he'd nipped a bite of nose from one of the sleeping twins. Human meat was gruel to such filth as him. I skittered up, silent as an eel, but when I pounced, his smelly spot was bare.

Old monotony, the stunted, web-flowing day, had me shackled to my toes. I let my head hang between my legs, my tongue hanging too, thinking what's the use? Why struggle on? This day counts for nothing, as has every other. Time, I told myself, to wedge myself up to a tree and sleep. There was hope for some tickle there.

I let out a yowl, a long, goose-bumping, arching flight of woe (pure bravado), just to show the world I still knew how. No one noticed. No one, for all I knelled, even heard.

I dropped down and dozed.

Or was about to when my bloodmate Terry, unhinged sister of mine and half-cousin to a sow, came bleaping through a break in the mud wall, her long snout smeared with bear paw from putting it where snout had no right to be—and now putting it there again with all insistence, blathering as though she had lost all hold on intellect and more as though she were kin to a creaking quarry cart.

"Oh, Mr. Hooker," she cried, "you've been fighting again. Is violence all you know?" Then heard Wolf's sobs and toe-stepped her way over to him, laying warm drool over his flanks. "What right have you?" she exclaimed. "You've hurt my liefest one, Wolfsleach, you hotbreath pooch!" And let loose a string of livid abuse, tying up my head and the air around me with her prassy talk, when here she was in her harlotry bloom, shame as far away from her hanging belly as cart horse could run or lickety be split, and the whole wide world from Shottery to Snitterfield to see what she'd let that snaggle-tooth do to her.

"Swallow a tod of wool next time," I told this grass-roller. "Oh, Terry, what's to be done with you, what would our own Mam and bloodspit say?" For truly her wantonness made me blush; she made me wish I'd shared my birthing with a needle-eyed snake.

"Poor Wolf," she said to the freak and commenced licking him from head to tail.

Inside the house, one of the babies began to squall, and then the other, and much caterwauling from the three women there, and next was the Hathaway at the door kicking up her skirts and throwing up a swirl of fists at Will's shuttered aperture, crying in her shrillest: "You there, rhymer, in your swaddling clothes, come down and change a diaper!"

A hex moved over the house like a savage wand. I melted down inside a pile of leaves, soul-weary and purposeless as a thing reduced to lead. My former cock-stomping was now all fencepost and briar, a honey's drip; I was deep in my humors and under my Two Foot master's unmasterly hood, as nothing had been going right for us of late, there being naught but woe and more woe heaped on through all of our long moons. I felt as some swooning, mooching bear must feel when the full weight of his cave has come down on him.

Madness, I thought, what's the use? My Two Foot Will was sore in the thumbs from brooding at nasty fate, while the geck's wife was sick with fury at his nothingness—"You'd take meaningful employment," she kept telling him, "if you cared about me or your brats. But, nay, you're all lit up by prince and princess, king and queen, you don't care snit about the real world!" The whole house naught but a stinkpodge of mood, of hurts big and small. Gilbert was a prance. Joan addled. Edmund a squirt. And the goose jar eternally empty, as empty as my clack-dish eternally was. Bubble, bubble, toil and trouble. My master's sire, the white-haired John, had the dropsy in his features and ever trembled now in wait of debtor's prison or the stocks, whichever grinning justice snared him first. This arch mentor, blacker in outlook than a chimney pot, spun out his daily hours sucking the marrow of mutton bone carried for luck in his oiled unrattling purse, the Geneva Bible to mumble over spread open on his lap. As he dared not venture of Sundays to Holy Trinity Church, the book's thick pages were specked with puke spewed up by his grief and rage or what was spilled from his dented pewter tankard that was ever deep with his and Warwickshire's best brown ale—which brew the young shortlegs Edmund, his last brat, was faithful fetcher for. No and nay, he could give up his senses, John Two Foot could, and pay off owed shillings as the turtle ran, but he would never give up the sweet mercy of ale so long as there was secret barley in the rafters and grey day didn't flaunt herself to final black.

"You're a tosspot, John," old Mary would entreat. "No more, no more!"

But the sour keg would go on drinking it down all the faster, weighing venom against the double-dealing law that allowed slagheaps on the street for some but not for others, bellyaching that between his loutish brother Henry and Mary's crop-sucking, swindling relatives, not to mention assorted thieves by name of Ralph Cawdrey and the like, he had no pot to pee in nor hardly cause to stand upright. From moment to nasty moment, he'd hight instructions to hapless Gilbert, close by in the glover's shop, although Gilbert, more fop than son, scarcely had wit to hold a paring knife and longed only to invest finery up to his brow, pirouette in puffed sleeves through the Bankcroft to Avon's mist-burning shore, there to sketch with other lazy swans the river's blue sweep or doltish archers at practice on the green.

But Will was the rub. That devious firstborn son was first to drive in the parental blade, and foremost one to keep it there. "Oh, he's for art," the gentle Mary would say. And stick her sweetened finger into the squalling mouths of what his art had done, for sure enough the duo's own mother lacked the spit. Will had no mind for wool-bending, for cutting and tanning, for whittawing sheep's pelt, goat hide, or cheverel, any more than he had for schoolmastering or articling with Henry Rogers, clerk to the borough. Shucked from that contraction now. Shucked for quilling doggerel in the book when he should have been keeping leets and law days and attending the assizes. The rogue. Ardent verse begetter, book forager, perishing between Stratford visits of ass-laden players, content merely to war with the Hathaway bitch, bounce his babies on his knees, carouse with that Sadler bunch, theorize on history, thunder at parchment, weigh the bait and line of Londontown.

"This Avon's a pimple!" Will would rail, croaking his fury at the unbending Hathaway, his face blazing as the great actor Alleyn's would, rapping her with sauce pots to show that his rage matched her ire and that a

Henley Street son could better a Shottery wench even on the worst of days. "You twilight hump" he'd screech. "Old woman! Cradle snatcher! Apple-john, Barbary hen, you drumbling, letharged pizzle-minder. To become the laced mutton, you'd have betrothed your patch even to the wheelwright's crass boy."

"Oh, thee!" she'd rant back. "Enough of your flattery. Don't think you can gloze me with your mindless stammer."

"Bate-breeder, bed-swerver, thou imperseverent, rancid mome!"

"Codpole!" she'd answer. "Thou woodcock, what stick is it grows between your legs that makes you think you can take a merry bride and quit her before the nighttime falls?"

"Ah, me," he'd moan, "I'd as lief stumble over a precipice under dark moon or sleep in a quagmire with hooting frogs as ever again fall myself in love!"

"Love!" she'd croak. "You call this love!" And she'd potch him one and potch him another and take her claws to his sneering face and whap at him with her stick-broom.

"Hag!"

"Word-blower! Thou shitted stool!"

So toe to toe they'd push and pull, kick and blather, swing-buckling the very hour down to its rawest nubs, and quell all hope of sleep, leaving the Henley Street citizenry to think Doomsday's great foot was stomping down, that murder and mayhem were aprowl, with earthquake next . . . until at last the tethered pair apoplexed down.

"Avon's the pimple, Anne, and thou art the blot that holds me here."

"Snecke up!" she'd say. "Snecke up!"—which meant "Go hang yourself" in the Stratford tongue. "Go hang yourself, wretch born to lead apes and women into hell!"

And this when—behold!—a fig's turn later they'd be all dovecote-trundled, honey-bucketed, cooing love notes cheek to cheek and chirp for chirp.

"Ahh, buss me, Will!"

"Ahh, my back's hot for thee, Anne!"

"Stoke me, Will!"

"Thou art a moist one, thou art!"

It would be "my alderliefest this" and "my alderliefest that," enough to make even a dog's toes curl.

Aye.

Aye, John would think, hearing his proud walls one minute shake from riotous argument and next steam up like a Ludd's town brothel from lip-smacking and what else? Gods forbot, he'd think, the plague should have got us all! Him married to that sack of hip and tit and three foaled before I could shake a stick. Now five here to nest, crowding me out of house and home!

Woe, woe.

So the pater would stare down at his wasted glover's hands at scratch over his woolen crotch, and at his legs gone spindly from what the physician said was disuse and nothing more—else he wanted the cure of frog's spawn to wrap his tongue around—and with bemused, unbalanced eye he'd thus follow the unwelcome oar and paddle of the world. His grief so thick he hacked it up in hacking cough, he'd wetly contemplate this cargo of troubles descended on him—humans of every age, drift, and treacherous scope, some two or three with mustard enough to capsize the walls even of a double house— and try to blink back what the world had done to him, ambitious yeoman's son seven years apprenticed to that daft Dickson scoundrel, cutter of white gloves, and then risen to be ale taster, constable, alderman, and finally boss-man bailiff (a good Lord Mayor, eh what? and privileged to wear the town's scarlet gown). A burgess of uncommon esteem. Not bad for a farmer's boy. And graced in the bargain with an Arden heiress for bride. "Since spring fifty-eight it was," he'd remind himself in a mumble, ale aflow down his chin, "the year a mule throwed poor Timothy Fox and broke his neck." Precious Mary, his nightingale, his hopemate, his nightly tonic. "My bosom," he'd say, "my chuck, my soul's breath, Mary."

Yea, and autumn the year before—"Or fifty-six, maybe it was, what's time to a sticklehead like me?"— his hand in Mary's as they approached her enfeebled old pa, swimming through seven sisters to have their pull on him. But no worry, Mary being the favorite. "What? Marriage? To this slackjaw? You want *him*? A rusty sharecropper's son when there's gentry chasing all round your heels? You'd corrupt our noble flow? What would old Turchillus of Arden say? Roll over in his grave, the bugger would. You do? You will? You want him anyway? Well, bugger old Turchill, if you say we must. But hold off a year or two. Wait till after I'm aged and impotent and dead. Then you can hawk down with him."

A fine, mellowy old ram, despite his talk. One of the best.

But what Robert Arden didn't know that day as they stood before him with clasped hands, begging leave to marry, was that the airy Warwickshire hills had made their brains to dance and already they were hawking down. That they'd stole their secret cups more than once. And Mary worried lest her tummy heave up and betray the stumbling. Yet eager to hawk again each chance she got. "My hitching post," is what she called his stick, and wriggled in so tight and creamy he spent his courtship wrapped up in a sweat.

Now cart had got before horse again and history was repeating itself. As he was to his precious Mary, so was Will to his precious slut. Something in the Shokespit blood, he reckoned, that had to fatten a woman. Like father, like son, Mary would say. Oh, that the Hathaway was sluttish was part of her stamp on character and no point in heaping blame on what was only being true to its nature. A bossy hamper. Willful where Will was clottish. But sluttish, yes. The taint of pigsty was on her. You had only to look at her bare feet and sturdy legs, at her hip roll, how she flounced, the way her eyes could make juice jump out of cherry, to know what she'd look like naked on a sheet and stir a boy's hot vinegar. Making no bones about it, lasciviousness was rooted deeper in her than the Puritan tunes she prattled. "Head goes one way, heart another," as Mary said. "Faith yes, we've known from the start she was shallow."

Aye, Mary had spotted where Hathaway was charm and where she was affliction. Poor Mary. One wondered about Mary: how she kept afloat a household spirit in these ragged times. Such a sweet thumper, so sweet-tempered, was Mary. Thirty long years his bedwarmer now and ripe for the tranquillity of gratified age after bearing five to reach this mean season, and losing three only to Holy Trinity's blessed ground there, where lime trees give halt to rain.

Aye. Aye and double aye. Now the Devil take it.

The Queen, with all her rubies, could take it. Let the bishops have it. Stuff it all up Sir Lucifer's roomy rump. More ale, he'd think. Where's my ale? My flagon of beeswax, my stoup of courage. The stomach's rancid, my ears flop. Wet my whistle, how else to survive the gawdy hour? Time hangs like a stinking fish. "Ale! Another ale!" Aye. For Hell's upper shelf had opened forth to send its gale, and you couldn't so much as raise a fire for warmth without having your chimney taxed.

Why me? he'd think.

And for the humpteenth time ask it of the harried air: "Why me, when it was only a gentleman I wanted to be, and swain to my sweetheart, with as many prideful children to staunch up my Shakespoot's name as there are arches in Clopton Bridge."

Then likely as not the debtserver's fist would swoop down on the Henley Street door, and his Wilmcote prize—the same Arden, forty-plus now and ragged as her broom, yet sterner in the discipline than he—would scuttle his reveries by way of whispered shake ("Wake up, wake up, you sot, you sweated hog!") and hasten him off to root nose in trunk or chicken shed or in crawl space between walls until the coastway cleared.

"Will? Will? Your twins want fathering, Will!"

"Will? Will? Stir yourself to bring in wood, my Will. We're shivering, dear!"

"No penny in the goose mug, Will!"

It had all come down on us, this scourge, no question of that, and making us bowlegged as if by plague— which in part accounted for the short rope I gave myself that day in Two Foot's backyard with my bloodbone Terry and the whole of our comic pack. Thus it was, nudged from my stupors, I could snarl and cut claw with my own sister, saying: "I don't like this bone-bashing any better than you, sister, but for what happens next you've got only yourself to blame. For you can't deny you're here blooming with Wolf's pus, without one thought given to our present reversals, to the lost economy of our good Henley Street name."

But Sister wasn't listening and, in any event, would have vouchsafed it was all in the nature of her heat to take whatever longpole offered itself and that moreover our name was rubble already and we'd best seek the grace of new masters. Which sentiment did give me pause, for that cyclop butcher Two Foot Ralph Cawdrey, with shops behind the shambles in Middle Row, had lately been favoring me with headbelly pats, plus had boys of an age to run and chase, plus much of his meat was sick with worm and green fly so he'd keep the clack-dish full. But pause only. My betrothal was to Will, and although his commitment now ran more to his squallers and to verse than it did to dog and he was more in the chop of sullen mood than the deepest mole, I was not the mutt to fly into more advantaged prentice-ship merely because his pennant was low. "Good fortune spends itself, Hooker," he'd say to me, "as easily as it renews. Once I've poisoned the bitch wife, we can be off." He was loser, I mean to mean, but I did not think to count the villain out.

Wolfsleach let out a crow. The prigger had un-shackled his wits somehow to sneak up on me and get his hound's tooth fastened on my neck. His four paws ripped bloodruts in my soft underside.

"My heart's nest!" Terry drooled at him.

"Murder the bully," said Marr.

"So you want to play it rough, do you, dog?" I said. And I tore at the crapper.

We growled and whirled and glob-swallowed fur and spit; we clacked teeth and swirled; we panted and ripped and chomped on ear, tail, and throat; we snarled, sneaped, and roared in a fury over the whole of Two Foot's garden, long since gone to rot.

I didn't know the tongue-loller had it in him, to tell you the truth.

Will poked head out of his scribbler's overhang to throw a shoe at us the size of a chamber pot, screaming his intent that we should hush it up, for how could he thump out a rhyme with so much clamor going on? I gave him my grin. "Bugger your words," I told him. "Bugger all." He was too much harried and soulfully immersed in the measurement of his script to take our business serious. Dog business is what he thought. Thinking there was in it something less elegant than the hum he cranked out. Love this and Flower that and other such juvenile twaddle. Aged Woman was his current epic, and telling the Hathaway it was all about the bliss of marriage:

> "Crabbed age and youth cannot sop together
> dot dot dah is dot dot (I left'er)"

So Wolf's fight and mine squashed on. What else was there to do, was how I felt, having concern no longer for the wrong done to me. Being wronged is fleeting stuff at the best of times, as Master Will would say, but a good breech will clear the air of hanging cloud and open up a fine sluice gate to chance. So I flopped Wolfsleach down and with a snarl and cry dug a tooth's tune into his throat's taster.

"It's an enlightened age, Mr. Hooker," the wretch tried telling me. "What's a life for, if not a little adventure?"

My sluttish sister amended this prattle.

Meantime, my brackleech Marr had retreated into deep shade, there to lick toe and wag tail, her ears flexing straight, her stern aquiver and rumped up in the dogly tease, laughing with her jaws as generally she environed us with coquettish delight.

She looked cute, I'm saying, and I could feel lust for her sex even as that mange Wolf was sinking the whole of one fang into my frustrated paw. "Whichever one of you gets up first, that's the one can have me," is what Marr was saying. "I'll make it worth your while."

She wasn't class, my Marr. She knelled I had a soft spot for her, and how to work it up. It was her very commonness that yanked my dogger hard—to which Will would say, "I know what you mean, Hooker, for in these woods man and dog are one." I liked her coarse features, her hair a russet stain deeper than fox yet not quite in the same mud hue. Her stink. "Oh, there's a firebox that burns our kind of log as we burn to fill it up," is what Will would say. Or quote me more aptly yet the print-brand he meant to put on his Hathaway, as earlier in a Shottery time she had put her witch on him:

> "Graze on my lips; and if those hills be dry,
> Stray lower, where the pleasant fountains lie.
> . . . be my deer, since I am such a park;
> No dog shall rouse thee, though a thousand bark."

Marr had the same strumpety incline. Her brain was fettered, wanting scarce more than my dogger's fast rent. "If it's true love you want, bark it up another tree." That was Marr's tune, and one that the odd trip to church couldn't sway her from. "I go for the dozing," she'd say, "and to run off with the communion loaf when necks are turned." A giggling, senseless dog. She knew not entrance from exit in terms of life, caring less where she came from or went. Some black hole, she'd say—if one got fancy and asked—is where I come from. Beyond the blackness, her memory just gave out. "Aye, but Marr," I'd say, "don't you think there must be more?" More what? she'd ask and look to the clack-dish as if table scraps were the drift I was getting at. "More to this dog's life than here and now," I'd reply. "For who put the hare in Cotswold uplands or glitter in the night sky? And, as for that, our Two Foot master is not such a shoddy piece, so who made him?" Black at the front and black at the rear is all I know, she'd say. What does it signify, anyhow? Yea, a cur, less brainy than a tick. And how could I advance her in the knowledge when our kith and kin had neither bewigged Queen nor eunuch Pope to lay out for us a beeline for where the greater glory was? It was the Queen that steered him, my Two Foot said, for she had Leicester and Essex and she had Drake and red hair that could make a blind raven dance.

"Life itself," the Hathaway would tell me, standing on my foot, "is a mortal sin." And swat me one, making sure her glum message stuck. (Will would drop down, laying breath-motes against my ear: "As empty in her noodle," he'd say, "as she is between her legs.")

She didn't dream, not ever, my Marr, the high-tail

bitch. Her sleep, that was black too. She wasn't vainful of her fur or mindful of her fleas and stink, and she'd nag you to Avon's other side to have her way. The time I'd first made acquaintance with her I'd been out scenting hedgehog at Gospel Oak, and I'd nosed her up and down, saying: "I'm Mr. Hooker from over Stratford way, pet-mate to Two Foot the glover's son." And she'd answered by her attitude "So what?" and "Drop dead" and "I care not who you are." So I'd boasted my town had six great dumps and two great clocks and three pumps and twelve treed streets, not to mention a clear-running mere, plus a fine whipping post at the High Cross what was curious for pissing on . . . to which she'd cocked a haughty leg, saying, "I can piss anywhere." So then I'd had to lick her up and lay on the glamorous talk and follow her piss-trail down four furlongs and a ditch before I'd managed a good squeak of her wrinkle-hole, getting fixed and half-done in my wooing before she had the gumption to say, "I wouldn't do that, Mr. Hooker, if I were you."

But I did, teased by her to give a proper wage—and went fiery and drip-drop in my dogger for weeks as a result.

"Something going round," she'd said. "Don't blame me."

You might think Wolfsleach forgotten, what with my blather in divining earlier days, but the dog's truth is, our battle had reached zenith pitch, for nothing rants the Hooker blood more than the weighty ash of days dead and gone. Our fur now incarnadine, I coxed him and he coxed me, the both of us down to drooping whispers, our tongues ladling dirt, barely growl left to startle a titmouse as we rolled kidney-bent through the charcoaler's pit and on past the chopping block and over the tanning boards through kicksy-wicksy Hathaway's hanging sheets and baby wash that swirled down like ghostjacks over our heads, our energies dimmed to forlorn yelps at the sudden flapping black.

Agg, what's this!

My head, I'm saying, was next to killing me. Wolf's ankle swayed like a feather between my teeth, my jaws too slack even to chomp down. My smeller was chocked with blood. I had rat's dung for feet, and my full left side bore no more feeling than a Spaniard's cannonball. But if I were so butchered, then Wolfsleach was hugging death.

"As Judas was a priest!" I heard some vexated Two Foot exclaim. Sheets were scooped off, and there was Joan, the Shakspere's sky-struck daughter, ungainly but of an age ripe for plundering, swatting past me to harvest the wash, driving herself to the task with the same proclivity a madman would have for battling butterflies on Butt Close Green.

"Wash a baby, skin an eel," she sang, "bake them fair as lemon peel."

Joan was complicated in her simplicity is my meaning now, for her senses let in little traffic except that which was good for her. Level-headed but liking to provide tonic is how my Will spoke of her, himself oddly calipered inside the brain. "In colloquy with the saints," old Mary said. Thus was she sound to Will's purposes, as she could be bent to perform whatever mockery his poetizing required, and warmed up his ideas like hands to a fire.

She let fall a babe's knitted cap upon my ears. And

stooped down to tie some stiff fabric at my throat. "Art thou a dog?" she asked me. "What's a dog?"

"A dog is nothing," I grumbled back, out of mood, "without from time to time he gets his supper."

"Then thou art not a dog," she said, but, smiling, let me lick the sweetness of her fingers.

"Oh, thy breath is bad," she said. "Hath thou no mints?"

"Yea," I told her, "at supper."

"What causes mange?" she asked with a sudden giggle.

"Overwork of dog," I said, "plus going without supper."

"Thou hath a supperphobia," she said.

I groaned. Her Snakespit of a brother would one day drive us all to suicide with his rancid jokes.

"Art thou in love?" she asked.

"Nay, not before supper."

She laughed, rising, then tuned her voice to another of the Snakespit's ignorant musicals.

> "Ere it be not love
>   Then love it be not air.
>   Be it not air, love,
>   Then I be not 'ere."

One of the scholar's Snittersfield ditties, tribute to the Hathaway back when they were kissers.

She broke off. "I pray you, then, sir, if thou art not a dog, sir, then be my goat and let me ride, sir."

The chigger hopped her full weight on. I whumped down, flat as dirt.

"Canst thou not fly?"

"Yea," I whispered. "To supper."

She unsaddled herself, crooning, her mind at drift toward some new and watery lullaby.

A spider dropped down from a tree and explored, as if for strangeness, some ordinary rock.

A hunchbacked cat was up on a far stump, cleaning its puss.

Droll Edmund, in the sixth year of his pride, stood at the back door scratching his bottom. Then he took station nearby, scowling as if on principle, sitting rooked, grandly gnawing on pebble or prune and wiping away on the back of his black hand the leak from his nose.

"Kiss a dog, go to the fair," he let out. Then laughed like a stallion. Snot-nose Edmund, the cougher. Unwormed, too thin to be human. But a good smiler, a throaty good laugher. The creature distressed me, as he needed learning, but I could see why Will doted on the squirt. He'd make a sound piper, Will said, provided the rats didn't get him first.

Will was up at his overhang, at lean against the closed window, wanting me to think he was hidden. Watching with some tension, snug in his secrets as a wizard.

I was too spent to give him a whistle.

Old Mary appeared at the back door, drying her hands with her skirt, shaking head at what Joan had done with the wash.

"Kiss a frog, turn into warts," said Edmund.

The entire family is possessed was my certain thought, for now Joan had wrapped sheeting around her from tip to toenail, with weeds garlanded through her hair, all to go duck-wading round the twisty elm, strewing flowers over unseen heads while intoning with fragile breath that almost became elegy-song:

"How should I a true love know
Heaven from hell in Stratford snow . . ."

Then the wench cast off her sorrowful spell, grinned madness at her mother, and sang:

"Young men will do it,
if they come to it!"

at the same time lifting up sheeting and petticoat so that her black patch showed true as a bonnet.

Old Mary howled and came running.

I barked what I could of enthusiasm.

Up at his overhang was Will with chortling big eyes and applause-smacking hands, crying out "Ecstasy!" and "Most wonderful" and "O Lord, my Lord, she's not yet for the nunnery!" His round face glistening, lips moving even as he fell silent, so I knew that now and all this while he'd been interring the maid's dribble in his head for liberation in some more tuneful epoch to come and thinking, as a thousand times he had confessed he had before: "Hooker, my mate, the play's the thing, and with the Queen's Men to practice me, young William the Shaker might reveal to them how." The prancer had vanity stocked high in his tower and went about quoting Ovid with a stammer and searching the abysmal heavens for his muse but he had the quality of the gentleman in his steerage if not in his features. "Stay your traces, Hooker," he'd tell me. "One day I'll introduce you to the Queen's lapdog. Then you can hump away, like me, with a royal passion."

But now the rogue was so lit up he had no dwelling-mind for dog's career. "Not yet for the nunnery, oh git! Git!" he cried.

"Come to it . . . and woo it," the merry Joan was

singing, lyric of the Old Town guttersnipes, our common
street song and tavern-stitcher. "Do it . . . I'll not rue it!"
Old Mary was throttling and kicking her, trying to get
petticoats down. Some two or three neighbors stood up
on high ground, their white eyes all agiggle. Hathaway
arrived, arms folded, at the doorway, looking stern as a
vicar, maddened that anyone could be loose but her.
Now John came running, stomping his great boots down,
sloshing his tankard. "What's done, what's done?" he
asked in his besottedness, flummoxing the air, spotting
in the end not airy Joan but dog at his innocent vigil.
And snapped off switch from a thorny shrub and, with
nothing given to justice, came switching it down on me.
"The dog's hydrophobic," he shouted, "is that the curse?"
I shied over, kicking up all fours, feeling nothing, being
already half-dead. The switcher switched and gulped
his ale and switched again.

"Kiss a spider, go inside'er," laughed the Edmund
squirt.

Mary led the trembling Joan—confused by all the
fuss—up to the door. "Inside, child," she said, "where
there's hard penance waiting you." Joan arighted herself
as she went through the door, touching hand to the
Hathaway's shoulder, laying on this last tune in a falsetto
the image of Anne: "Quoth she, 'Before you tumbled
me, you promised me to wed. Now that's so. So, tumbling me, you'll not to London go.'"

Hathaway fumed; Will cackled. Their eyes locked
in combat of each other, and I wondered how accidental
was the sister's mad performance. Whether Will had not
set it up in Joan to go at the wife's goose with a play
within a play, something meant to unravel their Shottery
history. "Art is life, and life's art," as Will would tell it.

The rabble had drumbled off. I got one eye unstuck, and there was Wolfsleach sogged down under low hedge, Terry at lick over him. He looked killed. He tried speaking, but his voice box slid out of his mouth onto slobbered twigs. A heap of ants tried running off with a chunk of his ear. Or perhaps the chunk was my own, or the ants invented, for my seeing was truly spiderwebbed.

"What now, Mr. Hooker?" said Marr. "I'm bored."

Them that squats to piss, there's no satisfying them.

I ached. I solemnly ached. My insides clanged like hammers in a wheelwright's shop. Venomous toads hopped heavy as iron along my stomach walls, spurting their poisons. Worms gnawed beneath my fangs. Unable to lift my head, I retched down over my standing spot. Blood and slimy noodles and greyish stringy ribbons of gut driveled forth. I heaved, and more string came, this time with a brackish odor. Ummm. I licked tentatively. Then dropped painfully down, slurping as best I could. The lumps had some good news in them—something mystifying that had found its way, days back, into our clack-dish. Not mutton, for I would know that. Not hog's pudding. Nor yet a candle stub. Not rat's head. Not hare, which was said to heighten melancholy. Not yam, stayed on roasting in the embers till it be as charcoal and noted for aphrodisiacal qualities. Not neck of chicken nor marmot's tongue nor acorn bullet. Not brain of cow. Maybe some goat's gristle unmellowed in the stew.

The odor was brinish and penetrating to my packed sniffer. "Good stuff," I said. I meant to breathe this only on the QT, but it came out noisome along with a sneeze. Marr's interest quickened. She padded up, whining

softly. I embraced the puddle with my paws. She gently
nudged. A polite inquiry. How you doing, love? What's
with the weather, darlin'? But I knew the hypocrite.
She licked my ears, meaning to distract. She stared her
eyes courteously into mine as she licked tongue over my
chin. Sorry for our little misunderstanding. She grinned
foolishly. I wasn't deceived. She wanted my puddle. Yet
her breath was so weedishly sour and good I closed my
eyes. Ummmm. Nice licking, Marr. Her tongueheat,
her spit, was better than any ointment. Dr. Marr. Oh,
Mr. Hooker, is something ailing you? Are your insides
rotten? In the natural hierarchy of medicine, first came
physician, then surgeon, then tooth-drawer, tinker, horse-
leech, sow-gelder, and conjuror. Somewhere in this
pecker's chain was Dr. Marr. Open a vein, cup the blood,
take good flask of my urine. Somehow the four com-
pounds of dog and man's life had got imbalanced. Overdose of phlegm, overdose of bile. Overdose of Dog
Denied a Future. Pour boiling oil down my throat.
Cauterize me, Marr. Pulp of earthworm, oil of lily is
what's called for now. Or set me on the gallows and
wring off my head. Castrate me and unhang me and
lay my bowels open. What's done for the rabble can
surely be done for dog. Cure me, Marr, and if death's
the tick, then Hooker is all for it. Let them say Hooker
served fit guinea pig to medical invention.

Marr's quackery was to other directions. She stepped
behind me, nosed up my tail, and licked me there. She
moaned softly. So did I. It felt curious, it always does,
but only for the briefest minute. Then the kettle boils.

"My preciousest one," she whispered.

Then licked and whispered more. My eyes went

rattle inside my head. Then with a last lick, she kicked —and struck for my puddle. Lap, lap, lap. Oh, good! Oh, tasty! Oh, Mr. Hooker, this is excellent!

I nipped her, but out of habit only, for unlike some dogs, I hold no great store for my slimy insides. It's soul that more interests me, and sometimes it comes vaunting itself about with a peacock's plume, such as those the clown Dickie Tarlton has made famous. A jesting soul. It had showed itself now . . . was frolicking over the yard. Some flock of birds in a yonder tree saw it and in one wedge swooped away. The very grass seemed to bow and creep down. Soul is an airy-fairy thing, with a cock-a-doodle-do for what you may think of it. It likes best—by my gauge—entering other stuff after giving your own bones up for dead. But for my own still-quivering be-hind, I might have reasoned it now had exited from me. Soul's immortal. Here is where I take my first leave with Two Foot, who sees soul as nothing more than cabbage in the pot. As rank stew. Who sees it as fixed between man's sunrise and sunset as fence is fixed post between post, or woman between cap and broom. Soul's nothing, according to him. As the body is evil, so is blood a thing to be drained out. And soul with it, if it's there. Of a body's fluids, there are only four, and no room for a fifth. No room for soul. Does a grave fill up with soul? Ask the gravedigger. No, it leaves only its booty of bones, and these of no account. Our very droppings promote a finer greenery. So says Two Foot, and harking it first always is Will. Young William. "We're good fertilizer, Hooker, that's all." Well, I'm master to that scoundrel on this score, and will keep on wrestling him down. Woof-woof. Bend an ear, Shaxpoot, I tell him. Listen to Hooker. Your soul is rotten, but it is immortal. Yet the prigger thinks he's genius. Callow youth will have it that they know everything.

Soul's immortal. A dog's eyes and nose knows it's there. And it seemed to me it was now at play in our backyard. Something was at gnaw under the latticework and I thought that's where it had gone. Then there was a rustle on the snake tree and I reasoned it was searching that space. Dust swirled a small funnel in the yard. Soul again? Getting desperate? Or was it only wind? The chickens let out a cluck or two. Was it soul streaking through them? Or was it now over by the wood-lean where fancy Gilbert had come to take his twice-morning leak?

No matter. Soul goes where it goes. Taking its greatest strength, I'd say, from dog.

Man's upright, and he takes his news from that. Where's the virtue? I'd ask. Man reasons, he'd say. But where's proof? I'd ask. There was a chain of being, Will was like to lecture me, that went from God on high to rocks and reptiles down low. Dog was with brute beast, a shade up. This, the natural hierarchy, as he put it. Reading it off, as he would read a sign on the tavern door. Questioning nothing. What's there to question, he'd ask, lest you be a popist, wondering why the Pope is in Rome, fiddling his beads, as he gets his teeth capped with gold? God had first limb, he'd say. On the second was divine monarch, beauteous Elizabeth, around whom vines wrapped that would lead her and England into Heaven. The vine's deep-rooted? I'd ask. He'd call me recusant, ripe for caging. On the third branch were those noble-born and on the fourth were gentlemen. And the fifth? The fifth branch, he said, was all filled up with Shakespiers, who, by wit and hard work, were ever grappling to climb higher. And where's the witless beggar and vagabond in all this? I'd ask, thinking surely he'd noticed they trekked Stratford Road by the thousands and made the globe with their misery the same as creaking wagon. But the wretch wouldn't blink. They are with the reptiles and the vermin, he'd say—best forgotten. It is not my suit, or yours, to modify their station.

Potty, the lad was, licking up his time's dogma as I would lick scented stick or glide my tongue over leg of mutton. For in truth, though I loved him, Will was strict in his conformity. He would rattle no sword at another man's destiny, for all was fair and desirable in his mind's realm: the sop hated equality. He would have echoed the rubbish of that infant King Edward VI had he been cotton to the persuasions of history: let the gentleman serve his country; let servingman serve his master; let the husbandman till his lord's acres; and as for those poor and vagabonded, well, let them be banished. Spade the hole deeper, roll the putrid rabble in. Will could see men hanged for stealing a biscuit and smile at this prettily. He would take no umbrage at innocent throats slit or widows set aflame for concocting eel's broth of a Sunday. "We are hooked to our stars, Hooker," the stink would say. "We sink or swim by their glimmer."

"Untune the lute," under breath I'd utter, meaning it ironical. "Take but degree away and hark Jupiter's bolts that would follow." He'd hike up his ears at the syllable-roll but stand dumb to their subtlety. "Chaos is odious, Hooker," he'd say. "Better a thousand vagabonds perish for bread than one strand of our Queen's hair be ruffled. Giving alms is laudatory but doing more is excessive. I'd sooner run through Henley Street waving a papal license as ever sing out that society's change was desirable."

And I'd go down on my haunches, not believing what I heard. For I wanted my Two Foot less jacked-up by the nose to turn it away from all of the world's misery. I wanted him less romantic, less besotted with words' double-turning, less in conspiracy with what his epoch glommed was man and dog's natural configuration. Wanted him less easy with the conscience that called it moral to uphold that we owed nothing to each other. I wanted railing and ranting. I wanted hot revolution. Wanted something between pig's oink and Two Foot's trashy whistle.

I wanted anarchy from Newcastle to New Caledonia.

Yet the rake stayed prissy for smiling, pleased with his anonymous, herdish fibers. Thinking himself super. A dog's lordly leader.

So I'd fasten deep bite on his ankle and carry my fangs deeper with his every shaking. "Let go, Hooker!" he'd shout, and shout it more until his face reddened. "Let go, you trollop!" He'd beat fist on my noodle and whap me with sticks and dance on one leg as he howled his pain out over the borough. Yet I'd hold on. I'd gnaw the priss without mercy. Grrr. Chomp, chomp. Until in the end he'd beg my favor, weep forgiveness, charge that he would give thought to mending his reason. "You talk sense, Hooker," he'd say. "Now loosen me. Oh, you're a jolly bright mongrel, Hooker. I wage you'll be in stockings and shirt, wear hat and a doublet, and have a seat on the council before your age streaks twenty. Loosen me, Hooker." The wretch's eyes would water, and he'd drop down to give me head pats, to play at tickling my tummy, saying, "*Please*, Hooker! Please!

Open your jaws to my ankle this once and I shall ever hereafter open my heart to humanity."

And only when he made me believe he meant it would I let my jaws slacken.

"Ooo, I'm hobbled!" he'd cry. "Ooo, I'm lamed. Get me a cup for begging, Hooker, for you've got me as bleeding-maimed as your lot of stinking beggars. Ooo, this smarts! Let me lean on you, Hooker."

And so the false biddy would slouch, hobble, and lean.

"The vine that wraps your Queen," I'd tell the swaggart, "has its root in kind nature. What links those branches you praise, where sit fools lisping blind indifference to half the globe's agony, is naught other than humble soul, about which you know no more than clergy or pickpocket in St. Mark's hall."

"Aye," he'd say, "your lesson's stern, but I've learnt it. I'm a redeemed scholar, thanks to dog."

Aye, indeed, I'd think, for what worth was a scribbler if his weight was not put in with the long march of impugned humanity? Soul endured the ravages of fate; soul was immortal. Soul gets by by hook and crook, by quill and by quiver; it seeks out all manner of things, showing its plume in flower bed or grass or animal or even a limestone field. It will enter anything except hedgehog. Hedgehog will fight its own shadow, thus keeping soul out. Maybe. I'm not hard by my rule, and the hedgehog to his credit would affirm nay—and nay again—to this. The Avon's fish has soul, though we eat them anyhow. But eating's not the test. The soul's plume lays the grandeur over all of life, which is why the witch Moll Braxton, even with her deadly sins, should be spared the mob's high flames. Though she cackles with her sisters around their pot, she influences no injury over you and me. The stars, I'm willing to think, might be another matter. What's stelliferous is beyond dog's howl, though up there is something ever pushing and turning it. For howl never climbs so high as dog would have it go, and many's the time I've heard it crackle and give out and plunge like a sob into the green sea. "And does the plague have soul?" I'd sometimes ask of myself. To which I'd reply that it was a stinking maggoty world in some regard, but that the true war was one with time. If the Spaniards didn't blow us all up with their cannon-balls and Rome didn't tilt over with stored gold and England didn't kill us with its queenly farts, then mercy would out and the soul's plume endure. Thus spake Hooker, mad as a sea captain, pushing the eternal wheel of dog's lore.

I stayed on with dropped head, studying Marr's feet as she slurped. I have always liked her feet: the hob-goblin tufts of brightness growing up between the black pads like weeds through stone; the smooth nails that curve as little moons to reach points sharper than my own. Her deft ankles too. The beauteous knees. She shook herself, then licked her upper thigh. The hair glistened. Color is nothing to a dog, though I liked it at that moment. I liked the vinegary aroma of her spit.

"Dup!" she said, or something like that. She gave a short, low sneeze. I didn't knell to her meaning at first, then felt a slide of ooziness along my chest. Spittle was spewing anew from my jaws. I shivered in my joints, thinking of John Two Foot's hydrophobic rage. Only now feeling his switches splashing down. Ouch! Ouch! Was I sick? Was I dying? Well, I might be if I was rabied, for I knew the Two Foot's quick cure for foaming dog. Burial alive, after the head is chopped off. Then head sent to Moll Braxton, who would stew it and woo it and put it to shelf with her jams. For in this regard, as in all others, there was strict ordinance writ out: "Never hang a phobic dog upon the gibbet, nor once hung, leave it to rot and drop to pieces. Though if the cur be of sound mind and not foaming but one that has struck down deer in any enclosure, then hanging upon gibbet and rotting till it drop to pieces is recommended and mandatory. And if the owner of said dumb animal shall not do it, or if he place stones in the step of others who would, then shall the said owner himself be placed upon gibbet . . ." Etc., etc.

I raked my head down on grass, wishing I had soap and water. Lye and stone, an ironmonger's good toothbrush.

A rank bird twittered gaily from a high post. I eyed it glumly, lacking the vigor for chase. Marr's quivering nose sniffed. "You're foaming," she said, "though it does not appear lethal." I licked her once or twice so the pride could be hers, carrying my smell. A few wormy creatures with faces like maggots were at crawl in my vomit. I put the paw on to hold them still. They cooled and I swallowed them down.

A spider skedaddled by, not far from my nose. Spiders will amaze me, for they are more shiftless than you may think. You will never see one spider running with another, or having fellowship of any sort, either with its own kind or another, and this is true for all varieties of them, of which there are more than there are grains of sand in our Guild Pit. Nor do the webbers have any vestige of humor. They are colder in their dispositions than a white-eyed turnip. They are of two sets, shortsighted and longsighted, I've noted, and it's the former I'd sooner avoid. But I hate all spiders. I hate them for their webs primarily and for where they put them, but more that they will always go for my nose, then give a squeak before I can throttle them.

But they make good comfrey for dog's bad breath, so Marr claims.

Terry had bounded off. I heard her notes sounding up by High Cross, alleging that some frump had hit her with a stick for no good reason—the Pynder hag, no doubt, for the Pynders have no happiness lest they can be hitting this or that innocent animal. Next, I heard her down on Sheep Street barking at a cat that had crossed her path, and I smiled lazily at her when she got her button scratched. She went from there down to Chapel Lane, then for a few minutes I lost her. I picked up her sound again when she was jogging up Tinker's dirt to Rother Street, where a passel of no-name half-bloods hooked up with her. With that bunch she struck off across the fields. Marr perked up, noting that Terry had picked up the scent of something. "No wind, no rain," she said. "The tracking will be good."

I was curious too, but stayed half-dead.

"Are you coming?" she asked me. I stifled a sleepi-fied yawn, which bored her, so she asked Wolfsleach. He didn't open an eye or in any way stir. Marr took off. I heard her a few minutes later when she joined Terry's pack, then I heard them running, getting more distant, until at last only my own emptiness came back.

I felt as if some giant, bubonic slug had got his foot in my stomach, making my belly drag. My throat was dry. I had the shakes in my hind legs. Even my tailbone ached.

Wolfsleach worried me. His form looked evil, like he had given up breathing. I had seen dogs the way he was, nosed up under rubbish leaves, out to make shallow trench in which they might with dignity expire. I stared lengthily at this gnarled creature, wondering if I hadn't wronged him, after all. Dog will be dog, as Will says. I felt some warmness toward the Wolf now that I knew his teeth were sharp. That he wasn't gibbish in his outlook. He had archpower in his veins—was still bletchy—but he might grow out of it, adhering to my rule. So he'd humped Marr and humped Terry and put her in a family way. So what? I had done the same in my youth, and done it a thousand times. No need to hit the ceiling or call down Jupiter's wrath.

Will was up at his overhang cursing his script. He flung his shutters wide and let out a string of epithets long as a fishwife's arm, then slammed the shutters shut and dropped down again to his composing. There was scarce no chance of getting the rogue out of doors today. He was a tedious, formidable hump when he had the muse on him, with no more character than a goose unfeathered. And he had the work piling up now, having made recent voice contract, with no pence in hand, to the Earl of Worcester's Men for a scene or act or skit featuring a prince turned into ass (or the other way round), and in upshot of this he'd been tracking down Holinshed's *Chronicles* or history for an idea, plus chewing on his toenails.

William Greenway knocked in. He and old John hoed the breeze for a good ten minutes out under the elm. Greenway put a shilling or two in John's hand for trinkets passed to market up in Ludd's town. The visitor was carrier of goods for the borough, and I had often chased his packhorse or wainscarte as he took off or came in.

"How blushes a mongrel today?" he asked me as I put the lick on him. He patted rough pats on my head. "You look off your color, old Hooker," he said. "You look tuckered down, like as if you've been kissed by a witch in a cloven pine." I grinned fondness at him, though it was his wife Ursula, daughter to Ralph Cawdrey, that I most vamped, since her meat chunks were thrice-boiled and had gristle in them.

They talked their business for a spate more, content to let dog watch, then Greenway said something that made my hair rise up. That made my chops drip livid with fear.

The Regarders were coming, he said.

I let out a quick snarl and bark. When he didn't respond, I put frustrated teeth to his sleeve.

"Regarders?" I said.

I'd as soon he'd announced the Devil was coming with an army of ten thousand brush-beaters.

Old John whapped me, telling me to loosen that man. But I blinked and tugged more. Greenway dropped his look into my eyes. For a second his stamp softened and I saw in it sympathy, understanding, for me and for my kind. Then it parched over, and he was talking Two Foot again.

"Yope," he said. "I passed them on the road as I was hoofing it in. Tipped my hat and passed on. But I got the drift of the matter from Raven down by the bridge. Something about a fallow deer some dog or dogs brought down at Sir Lucy's park."

My liver ran cold. For this was sorry news, if news it was. I pawed at his stocking leg, dire to learn more.

"Lucy don't have park," grumbled John. "What Lucy's got is a coney warren."

"Coney warren or not," said Greenway, "Lucy can't deny he's got deer. I've seen them myself."

"Well, is it coney or is it imparked? That's my question," said John, only wanting to argue. His face had gone red as poker. He didn't care about Lucy or about dog, or about deer, but he did care about enclosures. I was running out of patience with these two. Every dog knew Lucy had deer and knew where they were kept, whether it was called park or warren.

John finished off his ale, poking finger first at Greenway's collar, then letting it roam around to take in the whole of the wide fields. "If dogs found deer in what was meant to pasture rabbit," he said, spitting in the dirt, "then you can't blame dog." And I liked him for that, though he was drunken in his exclaiming, hardly able to stand.

"Now you're getting legal," said Greenway, drinking his ale up. "All I know is that Lucy's got a dead deer killed by dog or dogs, and he's called in the Regarders to take the measure of that."

I shivered, thinking not many a dog-on-the-Avon will sleep gentle tonight.

Young Edmund squirt came running to fill up their cups, though Greenway begged off. He had to get to his draper's shop, he said, before Ursula gave away the last cloth bolt to whatever Jack's face came in.

"You're rich," grieved John. "What's your sweat?"

"Nay, I'm not rich, though my debtors will be, if I

ever pay them." He spat, trying to hit a wood beetle. "Yope," he said, "you'd best have William lock up Hooker and those others. Stake them or nose them or, better yet, get them away to the country, to Mary's relatives. Keep them out of sight for a while."

"Will's dogs are too lazy to kill deer," John muttered.

"All the same, you know what happens when the Forest Regarders come in. They always get six or seven innocents before the guilty party's found out. You know yourself that's how the law operates around here." He took a last swig, brushing off his lips with a dirty noserag. "I've heard too that they've gone past coxing. Nowadays it's the gibbet or the press."

"I know," said John. "Soon we'll be drawn and quartered for sneezing in church."

Greenway nodded. He'd paid more than one shilling to have his Sunday absences voided. "Some shepherd up Wootton Wawen way was telling me"—he paused to pack snuff under his tongue—"was telling me he'd heard of a man—solid gospeller he was too, with no ill wind to his nature—whose dog run deer that was imparked, and owner *and* dog were put on the press . . . and pressed till they lay groaning and dying. Side by side, man and dog, like man and wife, all to save the Regarders' time."

"They get paid by the dog, so I've heard."

"Which put the widow on the road to barter her flesh for a living. Children too, I heard."

"It's bad all over," said John, "and getting worse."

"Another man down Chipping Campden way had his whole stock coxed. Some fifteen dog it was, they say. Which put *him* on the road too, since his living was all tied up in hawking."

"That so?" said John.

"Ended up spiked on Ludd's town bridge, his eyes gouged out."

"I believe it," John said. "That's what we're coming to, in divers buckets. Soon there won't be a wood left in which a poor man can shoot, nor commons grazing left anywhere, nor pot to tinkle in for the likes of you and me. There won't even be a thicket left in the whole of Arden or any spot in the realm where a man can take his maiden to unload in her his stoup of troubles."

"That's the truth," Greenway said, adding that he could see it coming. "In my old Da's time this was all open space far as eye could gleam, not a curl of smoke on the horizon or a field walled between here and the great ocean. If I told my old Da there were sheep at the door, he'd have said, 'Well, place out a plate of milk for it.' "

A timber cart creaked by on Henley, and I could hear three swaggarts' laughter wrapping all the way up from the Crown's alehouse door.

The sky had gone all swirly.

Old John was sinking into his pruned melancholy.

"Sheep's one thing," he grumbled, "enclosure's another. Soon the whole damned earth will be imparked or impounded or engrossed! You and me and all our seed will be walled in or fenced out, to be run over by bastards got fat on another man's labor. If Rome don't get what little we've got left, then the Queen's friends will."

"Olden days were better, that's for sure."

They stayed on a minute longer talking this blasphemy, then Greenway shove-to with his graces, and strode off.

The yard emptied.

I lapped at their brew cups left for the women's tending (John would hang himself before lifting a finger), but found no good in it.

It seemed to me some cry of doom had come up from the raw earth that had my name and the name of all dog writ upon it.

Wolfsleach lay unblinking in his death hole. Marr and Terry were up in the hills chasing scent that would turn out imagined. The sky was rubbing over.

The whole town, it seemed to me at the moment, raged silent, waiting for the killers.

For that's what the Regarders' coxing or gibbeting or pressing meant.

I wanted to slide on my belly beneath the house. To slide there and weep there and never come out.

The Regarders were maimers. Twelve lawful men, they went around the earth with their sole mission the crippling of dog. Stamp out the poacher, the stag-killer. Cut him and chisel him and leave him for burning.

This England, I thought, what a sump hole. What a muckheap, what an ignominy.

How they did it was they tied a dog down to spiked board, tied him head, belly, and tail, and they went at him with hammer and chisel. First, hamstring the brute. Knee-cut the brute kneecap to shinbone. Tongue-worm him while you're at it. Dewclaw the beast. Then expeditate him. To lawfully cox or expeditate the offending mongrel, you take out your mallet and chisel and place your chisel along the base of his center-most pad. Hind leg first, for this is where his vigor is stored and he gets his stamina for running. Bring down your hammer with full power and in one stroke shear off the center-most pad. Trim each toe up to the nubs. Then move on to leg two and do it most quickly. Maim the bounder. And if he bellow with loud barks and think to sink teeth into forester's wrist, then strike him over the head twice with your mallet. If the dog be especially riotous, then you know you have a dog of genuine sourness and no merit—so with your sharp knife give him quick slice in the stomach. This while you have held a pot under the dog's mouth to catch his gut-leavings. Have the dog drink it. If he howl in low notes and his eyes roll up into head, then you know you have finished. Take the dog to the river and immerse him nine times in cool water. Then let owner take dog back to his kennel or yardbed or pound. If the dog die and the owner complain, then be quick to run for neighbor or constable. Finally, if expeditation fail in eliminating the encroacher, then do as Pliny has recommended: on elderberry crosses set up on high hill crucify all curs within ten-mile radius, as this is known to bring crops to full ripening, honor to a lord's manor, and good fortune to all boroughs.

These infamous rogues, these crackpotted villains! Better they'd do as the Romans had done many times over: that they appease their false gods by sitting down to hot dinner, feasting on wine swallowed back by fist upon fist of grape leaves stewed up over biscuit of swaddling puppy.

Will stirred from his roost; his shutters banged open.

Our savior, I thought. Will can be dog's singer.

"You're moaning," he said simply. "Git thee to a pickle factory. Begone drab mutt. Snecke up."

And I sobbed down, quiet as a fat leech gone heady from his bleeding. For I had not the whatjack to tell him that if Hooker's goose was cooked, then his own would be long-frying. He'd perish a limp squatter in

Ludd's town or a rotter in Stratford, and be a play-spinner not ever, once robbed of the advantage of a dog's wide learning.

But now is good time (I gleam it) for break in the action.

2

ᐁᐧᐨ ᐁᐧᐨ ᐁᐧᐨ For all of this talk on the Regarders in Stratford that day, not much was doing on the surface. A dog digging in mud at Rother Market—to come up with peach pit after all of his trying—told me he'd heard nothing; moreover, that this crew was fictive in my imagination and long since abolished. "The Queen's changed it," he said. "Hooker, old claw, you're living in the past. Too many ticks in your pallet."

Nor did any other canine I saw give nod to the rumor.

Gil Bradley, hammering on anvil at his smithy shed by the mere, had his dog chained up and his jaws bolted, but that roisterer, no friend of mine, told me he'd seen or heard of nothing suspicious. A slow-gaited creature named Onion, son of a cutpurse terrier, testified he too had come across nothing irregular.

And that was the story all over. Though I went on with my upright sniffing.

Down near Old Town past the Sadler house one mutt, half-blind and crazed by mange, said he'd smelled weird blood on Clopton Bridge and seen sharp footprints belonging to twelve strangers, but he couldn't connect this with any band of coxers and, anyhow, I found his report unreliable.

Fact is, none of the dogs seemed alarmed, and most were too ignorant or too engaged in their duties even to understand the problem. Along the almshouses on Church Street down from the Guild, where death and old age and a thousand miseries were crowded in and smelling to high Heaven, I passed with some curiosity a woman in black hemper gown with red border and long apron, conveying live poultry tethered at each end of her shoulder stick (plus one unplucked under her arm), and the limper trailing her said he'd heard it too, though in his opinion it was naught but gossip meant to raise panic.

If there was dead deer within the county, he said, he'd know it.

I found a few dogs staked by the Avon, looking weary, but they said staking was their owners' custom while practicing archery as part of their home-guard Christian duty.

A lady, so filthy in all of her parts I took her to be inhuman, came by astride a square-backed mule, and though I sniffed her up and trotted alongside them for a duration, I glimmered nothing useful.

In fact, I gleamed nothing whatsoever in the whole of the town and saw no sign of commotion or whoobug out of the ordinary, nor any Two Foot strangers that conveyed the air of anything menacing.

The Quiney boy was taking his monthly bath in the river.

At another spot on the Avon, some triflers were merrymaking with the cucking stool that had been brought out to punish this or that unfortunate scold—probably the Pynder woman, for she had been dunked more times than I could remember, being by nature part witch, part scolder, and the rest dog-beater.

Maybe the chisel men took another road, I reasoned.

I nosed in at the Sadlers' for a minute, thinking Will or the Hathaway might have stepped in for a wedge of fat-chewing, but Hamnet was working and Judith was sucking on tube in the brewhouse.

"God be with you, Hooker," they said, greeting me warmly. "How's the judicious rover this morning? And how's your besotted breast-thumper, your sterling young master?"

I woofed it out that the bugger was scribbling.

It was while I was licking at garbage pitched behind the wall at New Place that I felt this roll of gaseous horror in my stomach, that I went tongue-tied, then blind with delirium, and finally keeled over.

I lay for a long time, tumorous and terrible, not knowing anything.

Bad water, I thought, when eventually I hove to.

I waked up queasy, my mouth filled with dirt daubers, to find this young Two Foot, hardly higher than I was and wearing a loose sackbag. He was staring wanly at my spittle, looking worn out as a hearth shoe.

"Are you an orphan too?" he said.

He seemed empty-headed and spook-eyed, gone senseless from running and stumbling and trying to find bread for his hodgepodge ribs. I licked his hand, wishing I could help him, thinking if he'd throw me some old neckcloth or noserag belonging to his parents I might roam through the countryside till I hound-dogged them and put him back with family. But he brought from behind him a long stick he was hiding and he hit me square on the flanks. Then he run off.

I didn't growl or give chase, for what it was I felt
was sorrow at his situation in life, plus his psychology.
Now and then stragglers like him came up from the
main road, London bound or from London fleeing, hoping for morsel of bread or nick of good luck, smidgen
of changed fortune, or for whatever it is such people can
hope for after all the hope left has been lapped up by
others. They hid in empty shed or loft, by bush or rain
barrel; they rag-tailed down wherever it was their body
would leave them. Discovered, they got lash or boot, got
browbeat into puddles, sent to the workhouse, or just
driven back to the road and made to borrow that space
where others like them had fallen. Coming in all colors.
Sons and daughters of beggars, of beggar that begat idler
that begat pickpocket that begat etc. Former freeholders
whose hold had got ended, the tenant split from his
grub-acre. Rootless, heaved-up, and black-rolling, cast-off
rubbish of land turned from the arable for the profit of
sheep-grazing; descendant of manifold villages sucked
underground by baron's greed through the long century;
industry's effluvium; a slow-heaving, upchucked, enfet-
tered wall of transplanted humanity—the red-headed,
trim-ankled Queen's grim children, though she denied
them. Now walking road to oblivion or crawled up in
ditch to hug dog that was no better: relentless army of
trudgers trudging for want of kind mercy.

So, no, I forewent all thought of chasing and biting.
Better to chomp down on a rich arm where blood still
flowed natural.

Yet Will it was that left me grieving, as his backbone
bent but one way and that to the lofty. He'd not sit on
Clopton Bridge for watch of these trudgers. "If I want
misery," he'd say, "I'd stay warmed up to Mistress Hath-

away's bottom. Nay, Hooker, I'm drawn more to the span of a kingly ceiling, to what's at drift within a gentleman's orbit. My heart does not leak for these bilish bags of malignant deformity.

"My nose, my nose, Hooker!" he'd cry. "Let's away, my nose need's airing!"

I'd tell him it needed flattening. He'd hightail it away, saying: "Sooner I'd eat rats in Tewkesbury or slurp eggs off the breast of Hathaway as stay there listening to your bleeding heart purring for those dung-eaters."

The weasel had no compassion.

"Don't meddle with the stars," he'd rap out.

Though I'd go on rapping, and yapping too, for I had no sense of dog's dignity with him. The prigger had education. He'd had ushering at Free School, he'd had Hunt and Jenkens and even Cotton that had turned out a Jesuit—all trying to thrash-whip the classics into him. He'd had red-nosed Alex Aspinall, said to be master of art and a man of steep learning, pounding his britches. But what had soaked in was all slime and sludge, to a dog's true belly. The strutter knew no Latin and less Greek, but in these areas he smoked like a chimney compared to what he knew of suffering and misery, of the soul and its plumage, of man's most bloated condition. He liked spearing my ear with Cicero or Ovid, loved pronouncing on the four humors, on the stars and on money, on Nature and on Duty, on love for his dark lady (by which he meant one not existing; Hathaway, he'd say, having walled that room up); loved speaking on man's umpteen ages and his fourteen sins, on indecision and thwarted ambition, liked speaking his moon doggerel and of unframed oceans; got his syllables rolling as he mocked the flow of the greedy inevitable.

"Compassion's for what's imagined in this Shake-speare," he'd say. "What's in real earth, Will will in time reel in. But for now, Hooker, I'll not sing of the chimney pot. Defend these beggars all you want, but I've yet to know one who loved reading."

"I give up on you," I'd tell him. "Your brain's shriveled up like old Percy's mule. Your heart's miscarried. Better you stay forever in Stratford, drink your draught of vapidness, take your sleep in the alehouse. You're a ratter, a shitter, a pimply Snotspinner."

He'd turn jack-scarlet red, stamp his foot down, say I had lunatic breeding, that I was akin to mad dog and ought to be locked up with turnips or sold to a cross-eyed gypsy for one feather and a back rub.

"His Avon's wind," I'd call it, for it was there we went for our beeswaxing. The priss's views unsettled me. He made my gourds drag, my gonads swell, my very gear box drop open: I wanted to murder the bag. Of pain and trouble, of a dog's woes, of those who poked face every day into the world's hot burner, the rotter stayed stupid.

Thus I'd lay teeth through his leggings again, and afterward I'd go for long runs in the hills, baying my head off, saying to the dark world, Where was the promise if there was no promise in him?

Half the earth on doom's boat, I thought, and it is sailing right by him.

I steered on. No Regarders, no one running to chisel my pad and stamp my features back to rough earth. A raggedy-aged bear with wit long lost from endless pit-mauling was dragging his feet through grass up on the commons. Called Dancing Harry, this beast was—once mighty king bear of city and country—now giving lumpy sigh as he clumped his chain, ignoring as best he knew how his owner's poking. Both earning the odd penny from the laughers there.

I hated both owner and bear.

And I hated Old Red the fire-box Queen, recalling how she'd owned bears and bear-ward since the age of six, and how she was like to bring them out for baiting when foreign potentates called by. A thousand dogs' deaths I could lay at this monarch's front door, never minding bear. Yet, as Will told it, she was civilized and had even installed plumbing indoors that she might lower her bottom on something other than cold pot.

On Tinker's Lane three urchins were squabbling about who might sell their watercress where.

A barefoot woman crept by, leading pet squirrel by a chain.

I looked in at the Swan, the Crown, the Bear, the Angel, the Cage; looked in at Burbage's tavern, at Atweed's Cove, at Ferret's, at the half-dozen other ale-sinks that kept Stratford's fifteen hundred light-headed. I saw no mallets or chisels, no strangers aromatic with dog hair.

I began to think it was all hallucination.

Up by High Cross I came upon activity. Some three or four were going at Moll Braxton again, throwing dirt clods her way, generally aiming to drive her back to her hovel on the Guild Pit road, claiming she was witchified, in covenant with the Devil, that she could raise winds, cause hurt, stir sheep to befoal rats—that Moll herself passed her nights asleep under a board with them.

Moll cackled, bent her scolding tongue their way. Moll was frightful, God knows, with her hairy lip and goatish chin, the flesh beset with rough warts from her various dabblings with hex stews and sundry other of her necromantic arts. It was said she had nine teats hanging from her bosom, one to feed her cats, the others for suckling her imps and the stray child lured in off the road.

"Singe her!" someone rang out. "She will not be so witchlike then!"

Moll cackled, saying, as they heard it, that only the Devil could singe her.

A woman, herself with a cackle louder than Moll's, ran in waving a thick stake and scored Moll across the brow with it, then fell back choking on sobs because the stake had withered in her hand, gone all crumbly and rotten. "Moll's doings," she cried. "That proves she's witch, let's burn her right here!"

"Weight her first against the church Bible," some wiser voice said.

"The river!" they said. "Give her the sinking test!"

But Moll broke loose down a footpath up from the pump. She turned out of sight and—to hear them tell it—disappeared in the sky on her black broom. True enough, the old bitch was gone.

So those with dirt-clod muck-pads in hand set to pelting me.

I took the mere trail back, dwelling on witch, mulling over in my mind what fed the popular mythology of things.

At Mere Pool one of the Ainge children (fourteen in all) patted my rump and dropped a dry bean in my mouth. I face-licked him, finding the bean tasty to my tongue, tail-wagging for more. The next was acorn, so I spat it out, lost to understand the squirt's cackle.

Another spitter tugged at my tail and wanted to take doggy-ride on me, though on the whole they were respectful, seeing I was in temper. "There goes Hooker," they said, "hind legs dog and front part human." I didn't mind this mockery, knowing they were addled.

A girl leading a stumble-down mare was selling what she claimed was rough woolen from Manchester. She called me squire as I passed, and for that I went back and treated her to a good knee rub.

Hold on to affection's smallish stuff, I thought, for otherwise it is all hell in a bucket.

Up by the Bradley house on Henley, where lived now William Wilson the whittawer, loitered Ralph Cawdrey and his three bosom companions. Cawdrey was telling them John Shakespee owed him money and had cheated on property and how the dodger ever kept his gutter muckheaped over. They were talking nasty vengeance, Cawdrey saying he'd give a slap of premium venison for a pistol that'd shoot straight. They were all beefy-eyed and loud-spoken, near drunken. Cawdrey's enmity against old John had nothing to do with these breaches. John had fisted him once for throwing his arms around Mary.

I made a note to keep a vigil on them.

The Hathaway was up at a high window as I loped in, showing her twins some silliness in a treetop elm on the Guild Pit road. Some bird's nest there with three nestlings in it, beepers I well knew, having kept cat and boys with stones from them.

Gilbert and the young Edmund squirt were at chore in the backyard as I came in.

"Wash a baby, skin an eel, bake them pretty as lemon peel," the squirt told me.

Gilbert worked vague, no mind for dog.

Joan was in the kitchen rolling out biscuit. She shook

a lean finger my way. "Why, oh why," she said, "will you not marry me?"

I barked proof I was interested. The lame girl giggled. Marr and Terry hadn't returned.

Nor had Wolfsleach wriggled an inch off his leaf bed, which put shiver along my flanks. If you die, or are dead, I told him, I will have the bell toll three times, no matter if the keeper horsewhips me.

A vulture sat on a high limb not a hundred yards away, staring intently at him.

The sky inked down like a giant lily pad.

Wolf's death, I'm saying, was assuming a lawful reality. By which I mean if you kill a thing, then it is dead. Not to rise up and say, Mr. Hooker, I forgive you.

So I sped on with my culpable sorrow.

Here in the Shakespeares' garden in the tatty rag-end of the season grew only shriveled carrot and radish and the odd lay-about pumpkin. I squatted down, straining, dropping my dry knots into the soil. I closed my eyes, huffing, pushing the last lick out. I sweated. My ort-hole stung. My tailbone cracked. But I kept on grunting. I sniffed at it. Then spun about, trembling some, giving low growl, thinking I was being spied on. Though it was only curious guilt working in me. For my dump had the sniff of deer to it. It had the tangy ripeness of deer. It had a fuzzy fiber mixed in that a suspicious Two Foot might want to call deer fur. It had the density and color-streak. It had the wild, graceful odor. Making no bones, to give it a level scientific gaze, one would have solid reason to say, Yes, that's deer.

Aye. And it's a Lucy deer.

I covered the dump over with a frantic scrambling of dirt. It's not mine, I wanted to say. Some other dog did it. And midway my burying got hit with a thing so close to religion's vision that such is how I would call it. Phenomenon so amazing it flung my bones inside out. A deer spun up out of my digested mulchings, radiance of gold between his broad antlers, swaying a full ten feet high and white-spotted. Saying, "Aye, Hooker, I'm deer never to run no more, since I now am phantom, struck down in my tranquil grazing by a foul-tongue cur given by nature and by birthright the crust and claw of a sharp-eyed devil."

"But I'm innocent!" I cried. "Some other dog did it! (Woof-woof.)"

I couldn't believe it. I'd actually said this.

Across the way, down past Rother's slagheaps, another dog picked up my notes and shouted his own innocence back. Then two or three others joined in, all affirming, "Not me, I didn't do it!" Soon the whole hills were ringing it back. And I wondered was this, too, part of our nature and birthright or had we picked it up as one of many—fleas, mange, phobia—in the Two Foot's curse?

Alas, poor me, I thought, for visioning wasn't to my hankering.

I whined, though there was no need. My deer vision already was galloping away in a spangle of golden dust and airy-fairy wind-cloud. Bleating back these words— not to me, to whom they meant nothing, but to life's flow in general, to something eye-patched that resided elsewhere on the planet or among the alien stars: "Mark me, mark me! List! List! The plume's laid down and who will carry it? Release me, release me! Adieu! Adieu!"

I shook my head, locked teeth on tongue; sat enthralled and fixed, as a tick chopped his way unheeded through to my eardrum. Fleas flit and bit, thinking brine was stroking my fur, up on end and bristling. My eyes unblinkered, my heart charged full-tilt, my senses jammed over. "Adieu, adieu," the ghost said, melting away into clover.

It was gone. High time, I thought, to set my head aright, to fit sense back into sanity. Was it death, in stag disguise, proclaiming its virtues, renewing old claim on the living? Was this witch-world doings? I sat on. It was as if thorns in my paws, shoes in my flanks, had all gangrened. I was gagged in the stomach and slit in the throat, was bleary-eyed and faint-headed—sick to my pockets—and humming down with whimpers that rubbed steep terror. Hooker's cracked, I thought. Hooker's got tick-pate. Do something, Hooker.

I ran. I streaked down to the mere, came to high bank, dived off like a dead sailor plunking down to Davy Jones's locker. Splat! I landed splat in the water. Doused my head under, got my jaws wet. Said nothing as current slammed me against rock and boulder. As it spun me over. Ah me, I thought, yes, this is better. Let tree come down on me and knock this noodle back to its usual disorder. Let lightning bolt zap and thunderbolt clang. Ah me. The cold stream was reviving, better than tea on Sunday. "Look at that dog," I heard someone say. "He's lost his marbles." And another one answering, "Oh blow it, Ainge, that's just Hooker."

So it was Ainge, bringing me back to real world. I splashed and cavorted, swam and pranked, though yet saw gold before my eyes and white-spotted hide in my bonnet. Visioning is not appropriate for dog, I thought; seeing vision is the Two Foot's mantle. No, not for Hooker these churchly experiences. Best I dog it away and tell someone. Tell the Queen, she's divinely rooted. Tell the church master, tell the alderman or school-teacher. Tell Ralph Cawdrey that he might shoot it. Tell Will, who might lay down his Holinshed and draw stage action from it. Ask: What does it mean? Ask: Why Hooker? Might now they put Hooker's image up on church wall where saint previously had stood? In niches now vacant, in the Protestant zeal to strip wall and window of the Catholic heresy. The popish baubles. Down with icon, up with Hooker. Down with St. Paul, up with sainted Hooker. Up with fallow deer spun down from Heaven in golden orbit. To talk madness about plumes. Plume, and who's to carry it? Without, so far as I'd heard, one word about the gleaming Hereafter.

Yea.

No.

Yea, I mean. (How stand you, Hooker, on ecclesi-astical polity?)

I dog-paddled my head under, took the mere's gur-gling water into my throat and ears. See Moll Braxton, I thought. Get a pax spoken over this dim cranium. Drink bat's wing soup, drink frog's semen, suck newt's eye and nose of Turk: let Moll's mercy foam over. For I was dog out of joint with lame time and ripe for suckling. With people in these parts, envisioning was common as birds in a thicket; for dog, it was rarer than molasses. Dog was earth-stymied, his brain briared, his intellect interred. Dog was meant to chew on fleas and confess to the world he liked it. To sit or heel or roll over, as master commanded. He wasn't meant for ghosts' skull-tapping.

I slipped up out of the mere, more than half-drowned. Shook water from my fur. Plopped down. Reason was returning. Heart ceased its knocking, legs their trembling. I licked grass, pleased to note its taste was natural. Only grass, I mean, sour and horrible, no specter, haint, nor angel, no deformed trinity, residing within it.

View was clear, looking through orchard, all the way up to the Henley Street house where Will's window was open with his round head protruding. Hawking words down to someone I couldn't see. Then the rogue got wind of me, his features sterned up, and he shouted loud as proud pig caller: "Hooker! Get your fleas home!"

So I trudged with niggardly pace toward these lodgings.

The Hathaway, kicksy-wicksy by vow and vixen by herself's law, was standing out on the back mud plank, scowling up at the sky's ruddy, boiling face. She had the twin gherkins Hamnet and Judith with her, one down wriggling on her hip while the other was up with closed eyes sucking on a fat milk-ball.

"Wave to your daddy," she kept saying, her mother-ness on her, lifting the tyke's arm.

My master's scabs, his harpies, his pudding and pie. For he was hung to Stratford for the care and clothing of them, no less than for the hugs of Susanna, his early-born and yet dearest to him. This latter lump was at nap, I supposed. Three years old she was now, a raucous giggler.

The hip-rider screwed up face, screwed up lungs, and began bawling. Will's window creaked shut.

"Squall," Hathaway said. "Let him rhyme that."

I shut up my ears, for the babe's howling was truly injurious.

Old Mary came out and stood a moment in worry,

taking up the squaller, staring up at Will's silent window. And by the sag of her I knew her thoughts: He will yoke himself to nothing, the gay, relentless fool. It was the Latin that cooked him, is my guess. Yet John, who can write but won't, said that any son of his ought to know more than how to scratch down his X. So we sent him to that frying pan they call the King's New School. I knew we'd ruined him the day he first came home saying "I can write." And next saying "I can't sit down"—on account of how the schoolmaster Roche (or maybe Hunt it was) had horn-booked him. I took down his britches and saw his bottom was red. Then saw it get redder all the more, as John felt double-whipping was required. Since that day he's been nothing but a stoup of troubles, and I'd have been better off giving birth to snakes. . . . Yet he's got Arden bones—my high brow. The rest is all Shakespeare. Maybe one day the lad will find himself.

The squaller was sleeping—Mary's touch—and she returned him to the Hathaway. She shook her head wearily, and took her misery off.

But she didn't mean it. On the whole she was on Will's side and stood up to old John who daily grumbled that he didn't want a worthless son, much less a brood of howling Hathaways, living under his roof and by his sweat and blood.

Though John meant his ravings no more than she did hers. Will was Will. You couldn't change him. No more than you could avoid church and dodge the tax or fish in the Avon on the bleeding Sabbath.

The same twin bawled again. The Hathaway rooked down, spreading her legs, shoving her loose nipple into the squaller's mouth. Side by side the twins sucked, their cheeks blowsy as a mapper's balloon.

I humbled over for a quick sniff or drop, and got kicked away.

"Foul mange!" screeched the wench. "Go murder yourself!"

She had temper, that one. She had substance. A kick quicker than a mule's. I harked back to her and Will's secret romancing days, remembering mine and the strider's night jog down the footpath west from Henley's end, over the kissing gate and along the footpath's haw-thorn hedge to skip, hop, and jump past cowpad greenery to Hewland Farm and the slumbering settlement called Shottery. And how I was made to stand bark at the door while they hip-rode each other before the stone hearth wide as a witch's breath, breathing flushed espousals as their lust gave mist to the rooms where others in inno-cent sleep abided: her father Richard, old and weak and twice married, with three yardlands and seven children to leave behind once he departed earth. A stately, mean-dering place. One would as have mind to call Charlecote Castle a leaking cave as to call Hewland a poor cottage, for their rooms numbered twelve . . . and this much to hip-thumping Anne's disgust since it was she, to hear her ream it, who bore the drudgery of the place.

"My passion's tired, Will," she'd say. "I've been down knee-scrubbing all day."

This after she'd bit his ears off and put scratches on his back wide as a cart wheel's rolling.

She was household mule, I am saying, and wanted out of there.

"I'm cold, Will. I'm spent from tending house, minding brats, feeding stock. Lick this bosom, Will. Stir up ginger where none now is." So her hands could coaxingly plait Will's hair and her tongue lay hot strokes into his ears and her full body swim to his: "Stoke fire, ah stoke it, thou demented fiend! Give me your oar, your staff, your rod of love! Oh give it, thou talker, thou horn-blower, give it, my fair-cheeked calf! . . . Ah dreamy, Will, thou art the dream! Give twisty Anne something firmer than your Surrey couplets to chew her wedge on! Oh rope me and bind me as thou wouldst a bucking steer!"

"Your harlotrous wedge, my Anne!"

"Aye, a harlot for you, Will, but for no other, as it's your lips that make me so."

"Anne! Anne! Rollicking Anne!"

He was smitten, having less to reason with than a red-faced ape, and more than willing to take unto himself the finer fumes of life.

"I am yours, Will. Art thou mine?"

"Aye, noble humper. As far-flung monk would strad-dle his harried belief and call himself Protestant! As Avon's flood would unhindered straddle its banks every-where to crawl over, why so am I yours!"

"Then crawl, you breezer. Thou art a word man to lead into battle a thousand mutes, but be a whisperer now. Murmur it, Will, and sing it true. Sing out that you love and adore your Hathaway."

"Love and adore and would pummel my Hathaway."

"Sing it, Will. Wilt thou love thy Hathaway true?"

"Will-o'-the-wisp, soon to quit Stratford, hath no way."

"I will have mine, you nasty grabber. I winked once

and you came running. By my faith, you'll soon lose your wisp and be Will to my Agnes."

"Anne, Anne, harlotrous Anne!"

So once more they pummeled.

And her teetotaler, lumpish brother Bartholomew thumping down the stairs for a late draught of cow's squirt, for fish head that might cool his fat stomach, throwing his suspicious look out at the darkness and bringing lit candle to lay out Will's ghostly face against the hearth's darkest corner. Answering to them as boss-ruler to the house, saying: "The boy's a scab hardly hardened. It's past time the scab trundled home."

Will, summoning his wits to say: "Methought the pus that was beneath the scab had gone, though it seems now the pus has returned and is hiding behind candle."

Anne shooshing him, but giggling, and dense Bartholomew cupping his flame, saying: "The scab has a tongue, but the tongue's split. What is the scab telling?"

Will, being gentlemanly and homely: "I know by your repute, sir, as by your flat brow, sir, and by your squat feet, sir, that you are a farmer."

Bart: "Aye. And what's your topic?"

Anne slithering off in shadow to compose her garments. To find petticoat that will not be found, and to dab at Will's stickiness that is dripping between her legs like spilt glue pot.

Will: "Plant you any rye?"

Bart: "Rye? What for?"

Will: "For the profit."

Bart: "What profit?"

Will: "No profit from rye?"

Bart: "The scab's a turnip. Very little rye, turnip, is

sown hereabouts. Nor elsewhere near these parts that I know."

Will: "Why?"

And Anne again giggling, or half-shrieking, as Bartholomew has never been a favorite, and Will's as serious in his dialogue as a parson with fever.

Bart: "The soil, turnip, if you be turnip and not scab, is best suited for wheat and bean."

Will: "Turnip-bean? Now there's a dish. Hast thou any? I'm a rogue who has gone without supper."

And Anne spurred on in her laughter, pleased to remind herself where and on whom her turnip has dined.

Bart: "What is your name, scab? You look familiar. Art thou one recently up from the sewer? You look deceitful."

Will: "What was up, sir, but a moment ago, sir, hath now gone down. It hangs limp as a fop's finger."

And trollopy Anne at this exploding.

Bart: "Thou speaks a mouthful, turnip, that is not to my understanding."

Will: "Aye. I've been emptied by too much of a sister's huffing and puffing, not to mention my own, for a man's stick is sweetened by his huffing and puffing."

And Anne shooshing him, for though Bart is dense he is not full idiot.

Will: "Some ground, I've heard, is good for wheat, some for rye and beans, and much, I've heard, is good for both."

And Bart, his gorge rising: "Thou art a fool, both thee and my sister. Be off, rogue, before I take up my axe and chop thee up for kindling."

Anne, blowing out the candle, pushing Bart into

kitchen and Will to the door: "Tomorrow!" she whispers.
"Tomorrow, by the oxen's hamper!"

"Aye," he breathes back, laying on hot kissing: "As
Hooker's got claws and a witch has her broom!"

Then finally to letch away.

"What think you of my woman, fine bird-dog?" he
asked me, giving thump to his chest and randy with
dipping.

"She's in heat, that's sure," I said.

"Yea, she's a cooker and I'm frazzled, my proud stick
drooping, without poke left. The brother's a sticky cockle,
but Anne's a fine forthright piece, wouldn't you tell it
so? 'Beans and wheat'—what a tick!—though as for that
the scallion speaks it true. Come, let's run! The black cat
shall not drink our juices tonight, what little that's left
in me. Ah love, there's a fine feel to it! This way, Hooker,
let's foot it home in a hurry, as sleep's tent is falling my
way. Ouch, it's dark! But faith, old dog, I'll miss the
mare once I go."

"We're to London then?"

"Yea. Once I reach ripe eighteen."

"You'll hold rudder on this?"

"Aye. As my name is Shakespeare."

To which I barked and gave merry chase to scratches
in the honeysuckle growth.

"As I'm a rogue, the dish would have me troth-plight.
'Will to her Agnes,' what a rub! You'd think the wench
would know I'm only wick-dipping, that I stride to it
like a merchant to his profit or sporter to his bowling.
But, ah, she's a sweet, greasy urn, and Shakespeare
could have it worse. What, Hooker? Lay to and calm
thyself. Would you have the full world crawl up your
nose? Good dog, that's the ticket, lick your master's hand

and tell me I'm not a devious fellow. Yours is such a shining character I would call it silver were not mine own so base, so shallow, I can call not at all. Down, Hooker, down! Let the wretched rabbits go!"

And another time in the Hewland buttery, whilst her old father was illing in bed and the household-rest were gawking at the fair: Anne with her petticoats hiked and her seat roughed up against the milking stall, be-speaking her true love for Will and general enthusiasm for his particulars, as all the while he pounded at her and snarled out reproaches conveying my Hooker name —for I was excited by their dovecoting and playfully at wriggle between their legs—and my Two Foot pike knowing all the time that he would regret his claims-making once he was milked past his fevering pitch.

Aye.

"Oh, Anne, thy lips are perfumed with civet's wash, heather's afloat to the rafters, oh rock me!"

"I'll rock, Will, rock rock rock, oh my maiden's bush is aleak with sight of thee, little Cock Robin!"

"Oh, dreamy!"

"Yea, 'tis dreamy."

"Where's your tongue, Anne?"

"In thine ear, Will. Now on thy neck, now on thy shoulder . . ."

"Oh, dreamy."

"I'm thy dream, Will. Where's thy tongue, Will?"

"On thy breast, Anne. Now one, now this other."

"Easy, Will. I'm sore with thy chewing, though I love it."

"Aye, let's love it. I'll chew soft, dear, you'll hardly know I'm grazing."

"Doth thou love me, Will? Wilt thou bestow thy troth to me?"

"I would lick thy heels, Anne, but for the summons of Londontown, for it's there I must practice my craft."

"Practice thy craft on me, Will. Stoke fire, my troubadour. Rock harder, rock faster, as my wedge is flushing."

"Ah, God, as my face is blue, I'm pumping."

"Thine and mine, that's good bargain."

Aye, I say.

My Will sopping low as afterward we legged home, him moaning that his star-cross was fixed, his flagon struck, his oats sickled, his bow unstrung, his career concluded. "I'm an ape!" he shouted. "Lord love a toad, Hooker, I've fouled things up!" Muttering that it would take kinship with the mighty Zeus to escape the entanglement of his devilment now, for the wench had secured from him the vow he'd said he'd never extend to one so advanced in love's maturity ("Why, the witch is near forty!" he ranted) or one who had in her heart so many knots to count ("Why, I bet the witch has gone at it like rabbits!").

"Do you think anyone's knell?" he asked me.

"Do you think she'd whore?"

"Do you think she's aged?"

"Why, the wench will be decrepit in another year!"

"Am I not too young and ignorant to be tied down? Am I not Shakespeare what's for Londontown?"

And I couldn't tell him that all of Shottery were humming their lovers' knot, that her brother's eyes were everywhere. That the tale of their wooing had gone past Shottery all the way to Tredington, taken there by Bart's croned wife Isobel, among others. That they knew it up high as Nuneaton and down low as Shipston and Broad Campden. That they were murmuring it in Evesham, in Ipsley, plus Wolverton, plus Hampton Corley, plus Wootton Wawen. That some were saying the frump Hathaway was desperate and past prime in her twenty-sixth year, and proper fit to be hanged for dropping herself down on a mere schoolboy. Well, eighteen, which was schoolboy enough. I couldn't tell him what my Marr's own ears had heard from the rumoring mouth of a passing country hound; namely, that the hound himself had once witnessed the lusty Hathaway feeding her patch to handsome Fulke Sandells, Hewland Farm overseer. Nor that even dogs I knew, alert to my interest, were arguing the issue, some saying that age spread didn't matter, that what harked in the Two Foots' world was the how and whyfors of their troth-plight. Simple trothing was common and stood the same as marriage solemnized in church, but for this alteration: wife had no right to dower and offspring no right to inherit. Thus, while Anne had got his troth-pledge by adept cunning under bush, on hearth, and by back door, it was the church's front door she now was angling him toward. For she wanted her offspring looked after, plus had ten marks legacy coming from her father on the day she wed.

Nay. Nor could I tell it that she was goose-egged already, for a master wants such news from his own gleaming and not from dog's. Dog has no leash to collar a Two Foot with, nor gossip to set true with mean repeating; our brief is to take disappointment as it comes and not to philosophize it with wattle and daub. I couldn't say in his ear that black cat was supping on his features now, that black dress and black scalp-warmer already were being wove and stitched by sundry Hathaway widows and relatives, in preparation for wedding feast where their color would signify to all the brided sow's early dropping.

So I licked his hand and merely whined, trotting four steps to his one, rubbing up against his leg in the good Hooker style and thus giving dog's comfort to his fresh young ache.

"Hooker," he said, "they would have me beehived here, with no more spin to my life than a windmill's feeble blade. They would have me leak out my life in driblets and sink down into Holy Trinity's dust with no more honor to my name than a hare's hind leg. Here he lies, they will say, old William Shagspeer, the puke, said to be a glover's son. Well, I will not have it, Hooker. I will run."

"Aye," I said. "The world's a stage."

And he petted me, perking up, happy to learn I'd got his message right.

"They say plunging three times naked in the Avon on a wintry day will rid a boy of his lust. Well, Hooker, let's stroll there."

Arf-arf. (You bet.)

"I would have trod the footsteps of the immortals. Instead, I've sniffed after skirt and got myself inchoate."

Aye, and bow-wow.

"Coupling's odious, Hooker."

Woof-woof.

"Don't do it."

Aye.

"Now I'm a pretty piece of fish. I'm sunk to the bottom."

"Aye, you're rotted, you are."

"Shut up, Hooker."

Aye.

"I'm a peasant's thatched hovel. No hole in my roof to let the smoke out."

"You're gloomy and self-pitying, that's true."

"Clam up, Hooker. What's for me now? I might buy me a hawk, have it give birth to ten hawks. Then barter them for a basin ewer. A good shitting pot. That's my lot now."

"Aye, you're pizzled."

"Stuff it, Hooker. You're no more comfort than a pulled plow."

"Aye. And over there is a black bird cawing."

"Methinks I hear it. Methinks its throat-rubbing is more melodious than my future."

Aye.

"The deer does not run well uphill, Hooker. This Shakespizzle can't either."

Agh. The wretch's glum bellyaching had my tongue dragging. I struck off.

"Is she puzzled, Hooker?" he called. "Have I put seed in her tummy?"

"Aye," I said. "She's swollen."

The doper's mouth fell open. He gaped at my running. He kicked at fallen twig, screwed eyes shut, and shook fist into air.

"Is she quality, Hooker? Will I want her?"

Next I saw him, he was spread down on green meadow.

"I'll take up the cudgel, then," he said. "The boy will be a father."

. . .

And now remembering, as I watched his suckling brats, how later—a bare three months from their last buttery coupling come—I and Will together with old John were made to follow on horseback the Hathaway termagant's insisting family friends down past Rother Market across Poors Close onto Worcester trail. Icy November it was, the shrub branches still and the earth freezing to my pads, although the chill was inside. Will hanging head, old John brooding. Mary back on Henley weeping. For Anne was due to pant forth her babe before May was out, and rife wedding talk was now long past threat. My Will had wilted and old John had steered past rage to bode late consent. Anne wanted clergy. Bart wanted law to make sure. Simple "I pray thee, yes" uttered between bedpost and sheet or ploth between lovers at the church door was no longer pleasing to the ecclesiastical view; now the banns had to be proclaimed three times on successive Sundays or it was Whitgift the bishop you'd answer to. And steep fine paid in court. So licensing and surety posting was our mission that day, plus exemption from the lawful rigamarole, as holy days were upon us through January's freeze, preventing any possibility for the shouting of banns.

A full hard day's journey it was, of twenty-one or twenty-five miles, and my tongue hanging out before we hung in at the Bishop's Court.

"Here's the place," said Will. "I'll stand with my horse out here."

"The seducer will run," they said. "The seducer will come inside."

To the clergy's registry office we went, there gaining closet with a chancellor or secretary or clerk, as he might have been, a good and honest Two Foot ten leagues past senility's range, who was fond of dog and much liked stroking my mane: "Eh? Eh? It's marriage you want? Well, bless my soul, this is the place."

He spoke in a wheezing voice, like one run over in the throat by a wheel. As rotund of stomach as the barrel that seated him, his eyes bulbous with cataracts that obscured night from day, his hands afright with time's legacy, mumbling uncertainly of irregularities and assurances of faith, of bonds to indemnify, and of blasphemers known to him so corrupt they would bed down with crocodiles. "Aye, and have a sweeter sleep of it," he said. Hiccuping complaints against his bishop's reform zeal and of the general sweat of his post, and other such prattle as to make a canine sleep.

"She's a pretty lass," this fattened hog said, lacing my chin. "Though a mite short, plus being hairy and wide between the legs. Is anyone here to claim the virtue of her?"

Will had a solid good cackle. "You marry her, then, sir," he said, "as she's as good as any dog, one that would lick pudding from your hand."

"Yea," this ancient said, "that she's affectionate I can see, and not partial to refusing a man his honest feel. But she's icy and wet where a man would want her cozy and warm, though wet too, if you follow me. A kisser as well, I warrant it, though I'd mint her breath before snuggling up to her."

And Will let loose another great cackle, shining his eyes down on me as if he saw dog's wedding to this antiquary gent a right proper deed.

I growled and barked to show the wheezer Hooker was spoken for.

Ours was but one of forty cuts on the docket that

raw November day, before us coming a vicar, Whately by name, seeking tithe payment from some lowlife in the vicinity of Crowle. And as our clerk was old as a mummy and senseless in the bargain (elsewhere would he have been feeling up dog that he thought was woman?), with walnuts in his ears to cut back the half of sound, and as this same vicar was blowing hard in the chamber with demands for nontithing severely charged, our dithering, wheezing clerk got mixed Whately with the bride our Anne, so that it came out on the license that Will was granted privilege to wedlock not Anne Hathaway of Shottery but some goose named Anne Whately of Temple Grafton, who did not exist in that village or elsewhere in England except in our old duffer's mind.

Which progress gave another cackle to Will, but sorely outraged the true bride's protectors, handsome Fulke Sandells and dour John Richardson, who next day thumped down forty pounds surety, thus guaranteeing to poleaxe Shagspere to his weir.

The wedding was on.

One week from the day plus one, their vows were church-blessed, perhaps in Temple Grafton where tongue-wagging was slow and the officiate was rumored to be but of half a mind and that half good only for mending hawk—or perhaps in the chapelrie in Luddington parish through wood and cornhill from Stratford-town—or in some other place, for all I can knell, as Will has kept sullen-shift on his vows of that unholy time and I was dog-drunk and chasing turkey in Arden Forest with my Marr and Terry and others in our crowdy pack.

But having been man's best dog at many a-such bell-pull, I can give the tune of it as I gauge it might have been writ down:

The garbed curate walking forthe unto the howse of one John Shagspere, father in lawe to Anne Hathaway, and upon examinat of bothe parties fynding them suit in willing to be forever unto deathe contracted, the curate sayd: "Anne of Shottery, are you contented to be this man his wieff?" And she sayd, rankled somewhoote by her stomachache, "I do confess that I was before now his wieff through troth-plight, and have forsaken all my frends for his sake, and hope he will use me well, not to beat me with a stick thicker than is his thumb, as is the natural law." And Will the boy noddid. And in strong voice confirming his manhoode, sayd, "Yea, so I will."

Agayne the curate sayd unto the sayd Anne, "Woman of Shottery, are you content to geve this boy your faith and troth and to forsake all and to betake yourself cloven unto him only as true wieff unto true husband?" And she did make reply with theis wordes, vis., "I am content. I am content. I am content," three tymes as was the often custom. Yet our Anne being discontent with that to adde: "Williamne is to my verie good likinge, for I have had divers suitors which sought my good promise and gave charm to my name, yet I never liked any one so well as him, and if I had five thousand pounds and six hundred horses to ryde or as many elm as there are these two thousand in Stratford-on-Avon, I would finde in my hart to make him master of hit."

And Will smiled in his sober noddyng, for he found noble humours in this speech and hade come round to thinkinge better of her.

"I will be his bonny and buxom in bedde and at boarde," Anne said, "and will be his close ryte hand."

And the curate stepped back in apprayse of his congregation, saying to the father in lawe: "John, wilst thou

now go hang bacon of olde hog in the rafters that this
union will prosper in the slact tymes and the bad, through
plague and pestilence and whatsoever begatting?"

And John noddid, and dide.

Whereupon the curate again responded, "Anne, then
this it is. You do here willingly wishe that the sayd Wm.
Shagspere and yourself might be betrothed and contracted one to the other?" And she replyed in sweet
voice, "I doe."

"And do you declare," said the curate, "that you,
Anne of Shottery, are able and willing to sweetfully
couple, that you are in sounde health and balanced in
your four humours and prepared at your husband's term
to produce, best you are able, his like image?"

And she replyed, "I doe, and so I will and shall until
I am olden and haggart."

Whence the curate sayd unto her, "In pledge and
token thereof geve him your hand"—which she dide.

"Young Wm. will you take this woman to your wieff
forsaking all other?"

And he replyed pleesingly, "Yea, by my truth, by my
truth, by my truth" three times in honourable respeckt
of John and Mary Shagspere who had so thrice vowed in
their tyme. Thereupon did the curate saye, "Holder,
whose hands here intertwine, mutatis mutandis . . ."

And theye did kiss the ground all three, then to loose
hands and William and Anne kiss togethr, with after-
wads huggs and cake for all the partie which with grate
pride had put all fowl feelinge behind them.

That lip-locking now oh three years gone in the
calendar fly—and Cupid not yet sent to weep his lost
innocence at the back mud wall, though often enough

sent there to cool his heels in the bide of a sweeter time. Their lip-locking hadn't lessened overmuch, I am saying, for each was fain to show they liked the other's better than their own:

"Kiss me, Will!"

"Oh, I'll lick and kiss and feel. Here's a log to lay all night on your grate."

"Lay me out, liefest one, as you would jam from a jam jar! Lick me, Will. Lay your log."

"Ah, you harlot, you tit, you wedge! But wait, I'll gnaw your hedgerow yet awhile."

"Sweet-talk me, Will. Oink and coo. Let your fat log flare. Trundle me up in our trussing bed."

Anne had hit for clean sheets, and as theirs had the repeated sweat of tumbling she divers time was made jibe of at the High Cross pump where she was like to spread her wash. "Oh, I'm sore, Will. I'm bleedin' raw. No more for an hour or so. No more until the town's tick-tock goes round." Whether sheet, rush mat, or brew shed, Will had no mind. Whether it was dirt in bed or dirt between toes, he didn't care. "Here I come, dear." What was buttery once was still buttery, he said.

The twins were having giggle now at something the Hathaway was telling them. Some tale about two orphan twins lost in the woods and asleep in a cave. How they crawled over to a wolf-mam and sucked on wolf-teat to their stomachs' content. How they grew up boy-wolves and went to the city and scribbled out plays. How their wolf-mam came and howled and couldn't get in. How all three died old and ugly, with no pleasure in them.

"So stay home and suck me," she said, laughing. "Keep your Willikums home too. Roll your big eyes at him."

I watched her arooked on the mud plank, knees wide to her gap, hair astraggle over her face, brushing nose with her grinning lambs. Giggling with them. Truth, she had tamed down some; her wuthering had mellowed some. She gave lick to my Two Foot's mood; she spiced his quill. Her ire when provoked could switch the skin off him. Or so I knelled, seeing her so good-mooded in that squat hour. What harked it, Will asked, that she had oaked in the time? Oak was firm, and unlike the elder tree, didn't set the Devil to roosting on the chimney top. Her growly motherhood showed she was part human and not all tough crow. Not sow. Not saucy swatter to his butterfly. She had seeded him Susanna ("an apocryphal name," Will said, "meant to show my learning") that first May, white-skinned as new fleece and with locks auburn as his. The same quick eyes, the same nimbly legs, the same flair for a goodly laugh. The same humors. Aye, Susanna was his image as sure as that pressed down in seal wax or looking glass. Nine months later less three weeks, the twins had hatched, Hamnet and Judith, these same smilers being burped across her shoulder now.

A pig oinked over in the croft of our neighbor William Wedgewood's house. The badger's swine on our other side oinked their quota of contentment back. True, these hoofers, lank and long in the legs and straight kin to the wild boar—with their easy life, their snouty greed, their hold on virtue of an idiotic kind—provoked my displeasure and disgust. And my jealousy too, since they were so much honored above dog. Unyoked except on the Sabbath, they nosed free through the town. "Shake the tree for acorn," old John would tell his offspring, "for acorn fattens hog quicker than corn husks . . . and pray God keep them away from the Queen's highway, to save my pockets more heavy penalty." The Two Foot yet owned half a score away at another place down Henley. Daily he did all and more than these glutted swillers ever asked for or needed, and to hear them root, squeal, and wallow you'd think the world itself revolved around their wet-holes. The winter would unbridle its wide freeze and we'd see something very much resembling our hogs' great broadsides hanging gut-open from crossbeams erected by the pigscote, iron scalding kettles ablaze all around—and such jealousy as our mix felt heir to was knuckled right out. "Where are your oinks now?" I might chide these hangers as we trotted by their ghost pens. "Where are your gibes, your gambols, your fat hoggish contentments?" And Will, brushing hair from pig's hide over the boiling kettles, would look rapt, fix on us his sorcerer's gaze, and take pause to scribble inspiration down—as we, mere dogs, burdened with lunacy, put bee to our trot, wanting distance between us and the stink of that scalding place.

A shout from the Hathaway flushed me back to my Henley Street stomps. A hole, wondrous hole, was poking through Stratford's overhung sky. "Oh, rare sunshine!" screeched Anne. "Oh, babies, look!" The babies looked and I did too. It had no more girth than a hen's ear, but old John and his wife and everyone else in the house was pouring forth to witness this stubborn sun's lurch. Even Will's head jutted out, exclaiming: "Now there's a sight to shore up the matted soul! Twopence will get you ten it fades on my—"

"Next breath," he meant saying. But before he could

get his word out or wager be laid, the sun's wink had clotted over.

"Good God," rapped John. "Come and gone, quick as a conjuring hyena."

Mary bored fists into his rib cage, shooshing him.

"That's England," crowed Will. "There went summer!"

Susanna waddled out of the door and down the step, rubbing her eyes, looking rat-tousled and dream-swept, her white cheeks bloated. Pouty, frowning sleep from her eyes, but sweet as a pear. I hopped up on her, licking her sweat.

"It's Hooker," the child said. "Thinking I'm his clack-dish, like always."

"Beastly mutt!" ranted Hathaway. "Get your paws off her!"

The whole mob of them laughed, both at my shy retirement and at Anne's throat-churning. There was Gilbert smiling waxen from the woolen-shop porthole. There was Joan studying the sky with her frolicsome face.

"I'm hungry too," she said. "I could eat snake."

Mary had her arms around John, trying to slow his consumption of ale. Young Edmund squirt hooped down to the orchard and came sprinting back with crab apples puffing each cheek. "Mrrfff-mrrff," the rake said. John went to splash water over his face from a leathern bucket up on nail, meant for putting out fire. Everybody was always saying one day the whole town would burn down —and always some to say, Let's let it.

"How's the rhyming, Willum?" he shouted up.

Will's head darted out. "I'm a genius, sire," he said. "My quill floats on water."

"Aye," groaned John. "Would that it could pay the poor tax or buy us a fowl on Sunday."

I licked this and that shoe.

I put a nose up Mary's dress.

I plunked down in the dirt, giving a good backspin.

I nuzzled gay Joan's hand.

"I'm sixteen and ought to be wed," she moaned. "Oh, father, why wilt thou not let me be pledged unto this rascally dog?"

They hung on it awhile, Joan and Mary saying how handsome I was.

Will drummed it down in a temper that our talking was distracting to him.

His Hathaway sat with her head back, off on some dream.

Her offspring, like fat muffins, were at loose crawl over the ground.

The buzzard off yonder in the tree got exhausted with my staring and flapped up to a higher limb.

"I hear at the market a prize deer went down in Arden Wood," talked Mary.

"Charlecote," said John. "One of Sir Lucy's, I'm told."

"Will the Regarders come?"

"Aye. I think so. If they be not here already."

Mary wrung her hands, rolling her eyes to her Heaven above. "Alas. Poor dogs."

I slid off to a side bush, pretending indifferent leave.

Gilbert stood at his aperture, waving white kid gloves dressed with fine wrist lace. "Fini," he said. "All done." John stalked over to examine the craftsmanship, then called the Edmund squirt to come hither. This meant the delivery of the article to some highborn gentleman's abode, and the likelihood of tinkle in their goose jar.

But the boy was bent double from the waist, red in the face and whooping up his consumptive insides. *Whoooop! Whoooooooop! WhooopWhoopWhoooop!* He'd been sick since year one and was a mite, squiggly, half-ream of a boy, no thicker than a peapod. *Whoooop-WhoopWhoooop!* Mary trundled over to pound on his backside, saying, "A little ewe's oil on your tongue, that'll wash it down." And she guided him inside, though the squirt hung in the doorway to croak one parting rhyme out: "Quoth she, good whore Bessie Locket/ Soon I'll have your penny in my pocket." I pitied the poor lad his illness, and thought again how little it is a Two Foot knows. For that whooping can be plugged out as easily they could find a man riding a skew-bald horse to tell them cat dung over soft fire or hare's brain cooked to jelly would be certain remedy. But no one asked me what I knelled. Dog will stay dog.

I stayed hunkered down. The flies were crawling over Wolf's shut eyes. He had a rip in his nose deep as an axe chop. His tail and hind leg had a twist that made me grimace. A line of ants was mapping route over his forepaw.

There was a rumble far off. Then the sky of a sudden swooped black and low. The wind quickened. Up at his window Will snorted, "Twopence will get you ten it—"

"Rains before my next breath," he meant saying. But the rain was already driving down, or hail maybe, and everyone was running. Flapping and screeching.

The Hathaway stayed on, still at dream, her head locked back, the long hair falling. Down on her bum

in the wet grass, leaning on her fulsome arms. Her
stumpy legs stretched out in the perpendicular. She was
fat, I'd say, and not lithesome, not streaky in her frame
the way a good bitch would be. Her legs split now, and
petticoat ruffled, one white foot pointed north while the
other went south. Petticoat hiked up above her glistening knees. Ankles splaying out, each saying "Honey that
is honey, I invite thee." The rain dribbling. Her box
open. Now a fine infinitesimal shiver in her hips, a soft
sigh. A long *harrowing* sigh, but soft, like the breath of
a puppy. Her mound, all but invisibly, rising. The rain
dribbling. Ah, yes, though a woman's weedy patch has
appeal for any dog, this dog is no fool. The spreaded
legs is a cup without water. It is scent and warmness,
the heathery beguiling, the guiltless bargaining; glimpse,
while humping, of soul enduring the long hereafter—
this that a dog romps toward. But, espying the Hathaway, I could warrant her patch bespoke a gross aesthetic
value. It had warmth too, and a certain beguiling. I
could perceive the Two Foot's hunger for a friendly
annointing. Wedge seemed to say "Honey that is honey,
I can fix *all* that is troublesome to thee, and do it to thy
liking." I could see Will's regular summoning. Could
see how Anne (for what was Anne was wedge and what
was wedge was Anne, down to the wink of her eyelids
and the crook of her finger) had his chest stove up, his
eyes lidded, his breath rasping, his spirit leapfrogging,
as with a poet's sensibility he engorged the matter. And
how, chimney and cheek, he would be steered toward
it. Saying "Honey that is honey, I would enter." How,
in this surrender, he might say, Screw be it to Londontown. Screw playacting. Screw a scop's fine writing. The
Devil take my words, take *all* words, and all good learn-

ing. As honey is honey and I am *all* honey, why so would I enter.

Yea. Oh, yea.

For Anne pulled him to her, that I could see, like a lock to key or bee to flower. Mindless it was, to no avail it was, but useless to fight it.

"Honey, I am at thy gate, and would enter."

"Then enter."

Witness now, as an instance. Now some brand of lazy smile played upon Anne's face. The rain drizzled. Her bosom hove up. Her chin and shoulders arched. Her knees lifted. The wedge tightened. She moaned louder. The knees widened. She stretched, yawned slowly; thrust out her womanliness with a filthy bumple and grind. Groaned. Licked her lips like a hellion. Cupped breasts in her hands. Shook rain pearls from her shoulders. Groaned more fiercely still. And now—now sighed back down, easy, softly breathing, her mouth open wide as a bucket.

Now I would enter you, she seemed to be saying. Now we would be honey upon honey.

And Will, I knew, was watching. He saw this. Up at his overhang, he, recusant voyeur, was not dumb to the Hathaway wizardry. His eyes lidded. His chest swollen. His hands aquiver over his pulsing crocus. Steering toward his temptress even as, with abrupt, urgent voice, he tried raking stern rebuke down on her: "The brats, Anne! The brats! Fetch the brats!"

True, this needed doing. The brats needed desperate tending. For Susanna was knee-bent and pie-building in that spot by the mud wall where chamber pots—when not unloaded into the street—were like to be emptied, and where, of dark nights, one piddled. Hamnet had crawled over open hole in the loose boards of the tannery pit, there sitting at loose ends and at wobbly pitch, giggling at some merriment found in the darkness below. And Judith, the speed-crawler, rank with curiosity, was down in the far orchard corner, goo-eyeing some roving, pink-eyed, snouted, short-haired imbecilic sow that would eat anything, and was, with interest, oinking her. I had been with half a mind only to their doings, trying with furtive digging to insinuate Wolfsleach under a leafy crypt, that none might note his absence. To hide his murdered bones away. Thus I had already his rear haunches covered, and his hind feet, and was working up to graveyarding his shoulders.

"Chase hog, Hooker!" Will hollered.

And Anne hollered too, in panic and yodeling her horror, as she snatched up Hamnet just as the crier was tumbling.

But I was already up and streaking, and the sow running.

The rain kept on falling. A skyful of mongrels, unabashedly pissing.

But here, I knell, the eye is staking claim for respite, and so I will tarry.

3

The rain-splash went on for most an hour. During that time Marr and Terry land-lubbered in, drenched to their cockles. They went first to the clack-dish, then to Wolf, then to me, repining in my dirt hole under the kitchen.

"Have fun?" I said.

Aye.

"Catch anything?"

Nay.

"Come close?"

Aye.

"Rabbit?"

Aye.

"Squirrel?"

Aye.

"Hedgehog?"

Maybe.

Chilled somewhat, they lay in a curve together, licking paw and—between my questioning—engaging in whispers. They wore a strained, reproachful character, one that blinked stolid disapprobation.

"Deer?" I asked.

They exchanged quick glances. Marr cleared her throat but, at a nudge from Terry, stayed silent.

"No deer?" I said.

Terry got up, stretching. She yawned and plopped back down. Marr chased a flea up from her withers down to her dewlap, then lost it behind her ear.

"I feel rotten," she grumbled. "I feel an ill wind blowing."

"How far did you get?" I asked.

Again they locked eye with each other.

"Not so far as Charlecote," said Marr. "Not so far as Lucy's."

Terry giggled nervously. Marr slapped an irritable paw on her.

"Wolf looks half-buried," said Marr. "Why has he stayed out in the rain?"

I shuddered. The rain had washed much of the dirt and leaves off the bugger. He looked flat and cold and rigored.

"We met other dogs," Marr offered. Her voice was low and circumspect, like one bound by breeding to make her way gently.

"That follows," I said.

"Some ten or twenty," she added.

"Or fifty or a hundred," I said, "for we know your counting's not regular."

"More than ten," Terry inserted.

"They had news," Marr said.

I waited. I knew they'd learned something.

"News?"

"A dog up by Ingon and another over by Snitterfield couldn't hush up. They were all lit up about it."

I watched her eyes, which wouldn't look at me.

"Yes?"

Aye.

"So what was their news? Had they treed a cat? Had they been put to work turning a spit?"

Marr huffed up. She didn't like my bland derision.

"If you must know," she said, "they were talking deer."

"Deer? Dear me, not deer."

"They were saying one of Lucy's fell. That a dog of a certain known description, much given to superfluous airs and thinking himself better than dog . . . that such an animal brought down Sir Lucy's deer and tore him open to his belly flanks."

"Without bringing us any," said Terry. "Without telling us where."

"And this dog," I said, brazening it out, though my insides were at shrivel, thinking this hunt was a thing gone unwitnessed, "did he have a name?"

Marr glared. Terry quit her pawticking to shove nose into dirt and look offended.

"You could have told us, Mr. Hooker. You could have let us go with you."

"Go? Go where?"

Marr kicked me.

"Stop it!" she said, losing temper now. "That Ingon dog saw you. Saw you burying a bone up by Charlecote creek. Saw you legging back here with deer meat in your mouth."

"That was chipmunk," I said. "Chipmunk that had been dead a year."

Marr scoffed at this. "Chipmunk don't grow in this

part of the world, as you know very well. You must think us stupid. You must think us dumb as spaniels."

"It was partridge, then. So wormy I couldn't eat it."

This notion rankled them. They guffawed and gave dry belch, they scratched and shook and stiffened tail, they let loose a potpourri of bad air. They whined and bitched and said I was a liar.

"You did it," they said. "That's how come you've not fussed that our clack-dish has gone three days empty."

Yea, I thought, three or four, four or twenty.

"And there's punishment coming, Mr. Hooker," wept Terry. "That Snitterfield dog heard it from Sir Lucy's own mouth."

Dust was sifting down on my head from the creaky kitchen floor. Will's walk, it was. The rogue was finally stirring. I let out a joyous yelp, striking my noggin on a crossbeam as I scooted out for greeting.

"You've betrayed us, Mr. Hooker," neighed Terry. "We hope you hang."

"We'll rat on you," flung out Marr. "We'll tell the first Two Foot that asks."

My sheik Shakespeare, when I come out whining from splinters in my brain, was hunkered down on the back-door plank beside his Anne of Shottery. I dashed over to slobber affection's worth on him.

"Ah, Hooker," he said, first with sour grin, then warming. "Here's Hooker, who has broken his elbows at many a church door." The lick laughed. He meant, in his fooling, that I was a dog given up to rancorous living and would have to skip my sleep in peaceful Heaven.

"Ah, Hooker." He grinned. "When you walk down Henley, if you spit, as a gentleman would, do you then tread your phlegm underfoot, as is true for a gentleman's character?"

The piece was pulling my ears, tousling my head, near-killing me with his side-belly pats.

Anne was weeping.

One of the twins, Judith it was, crawled up to the open back door, and stayed there examining the descent, hanging by the grace of her gnomish smile.

"Ah, Hooker," sighed Will. "Isn't she a jolly right bedbug?"

Anne let out another string of tears. She sat haunched over, pulling away from him, melancholy as a door mat.

"Cad. Chiseler," she moaned.

"Ah, Hooker," Will voiced low. "Let's go us to Londontown."

I barked "Aye!" and "Aye!" and "Aye!" again, all a-tug at his sleeve.

The Hathaway was come over with the tremors. Her face boiled red. She bit both fists with her teeth. Her feet worked out a fierce rhythm on the soaked ground.

"My Venus-ball," Will said, taking up dumpling Judith, settling a tide of kisses on her throat and face, with tickles over her round belly. "My love-acorn," he crooned. "My measuring stick," She slung her own baby talk out at him. Bah-bah doo-dah pa-pa—which is how it sounded to me. Though Will gave appearance of understanding. "How do I write, little Judith? Why, I soften my pen with spit, then rub it against my coat." Bla-bla, she said. "And how did it go? Why, today, little darling, I went at it like a dice player. My words flowed evenly as money in a tippling house."

They cooed at each other.

The kicksy-wicksy was now openly bawling. Her head was down to her feet like a hog to its slops. Now and then she flung a cuss word out.

Then I saw the tears in Will's eyes too and glommed on that he and the Missis had been having themselves a serious rub.

"Stay, Will," she pleaded. "Sayest thou may."

"Oh, Anne. Anne Anne Anne!"

"One more month," she begged. "Then with my blessings go."

"Oh, Anne. So thou hast been arguing since 1582."

"Why, Will? Why leave us?"

"Sir Hugh Clopton, Stratford son, ponied into London and became Lord Mayor. He returned a fortune in his pocket and beautified our Guild Hall and built our great bridge. Renown is money and I have talent beside."

"Thy fortune is with me and my bed-spawn, Will."

"Richard Field, my ink-horn mate at King's New School, has wed the Frenchwoman wife of Vautrollier the printer, in Blackfriars, and become lauded printer himself. He has bade me issue myself."

"This is olden stuff, Will. Stay! Stay!"

"My Latin-runt at King's School, William Smith, is long past Exeter College, only Stratford boy of my birth-year to stake himself to university's learning post. This galls me, Anne. *Veni, vidi, vici*: I would that I had murdered the priss. Even my feather-mate, Adrian Tyler, him that was disfigured by horse and unable to distinguish right foot from left, is a Ludd's town singer."

"London's the plague, Will."

"The egg must to its hatch, my pretty."

"I shiver. London's grubby, a dewlap, a cowpad, a

quagmire, a stench. Thou wilt give thyself up to riotous living and make thy bed on Harlot's Row."

"Naw. London's the Queen. Even her lapdog applauds a good play."

"Thou desires merely to quit me. Thou hath settled I honeyed my trap with false breathing to woo thee."

"Aye, 'tis true. But Shakespeare's a merry lad and will not blame thee."

"You lice! Thou art a licey one to say so."

"Nay, I'm pure."

"I loved and do love you, Will."

"And double the round. But I and Hooker must go."

"It's that cur's doings. You would follow his rear end anywhere."

"Nay. Your rear end, Anne."

"Then stay and follow it. Be more than impotent soothsayer."

"I'll tumble thee, Anne. I'll wedge thee a thousand times."

"Then do it, hot mouth."

"You're the hot one, Anne."

"Yea, by my troth, I'm hot, and would lay a birch across your brow. I'd open up your piddling stuffings and feed it to cawing crow. You wretch! You oinker, you pig! You'd steer it to London and there warm your legs under a whore's webbed feet. As I know you, I know you would."

"Nay, I'd reek pure. I would be faithful as the bird is to keep wing, and return to my roots the inch my standard was won. My feet would stroke the dactyl and not whore. I'd thicken the iambic purse. Dot-dot-dah and dot-dot-dah I'd slap out . . . and Anne—"

"What?"

"I'd fly my wages home."

"How much?"

"Why, all that I earned, less my bed and board."

"You'd a stranger be."

"Nay. In summer the theater shuts. I could come home then."

"Not if you were minstrel-frocked."

"Minstrels, fie! Fo and fum, I would pen grander stuff and can do it, Anne, with as much mettle as I done you."

"Thy vanity is the more-erected poke."

"Neither vanity nor poke, nor anything else I've seen, can soothe a minded Hath-her-way."

"Your father speaks that he went to London once. It's a bargain, he tells, if it's madness you want."

"Am I to London, then? Do I have leave?"

"In the next month or two, after your baby's teeth have in."

"Oh, screw you, Anne, you horror, you doxie, you hag's tooth, you crone and chimney sweep! You'd have me stay my career for a brat's tooth? Why not for a sow's ear? Why not for a maggot's tit? Ah, I know you, you'd have me rot here with no more virtue than a hunchback swine."

"If thou art the swine, then stay and swill me. Stay, Will."

"Nay, nay, nay. I will go out and bludgeon sheep. I will see Moll Braxton and have her mount my head to an ass's four legs that you might better ride me and rule me and my mule droppings. What's pride, what's wanting, what's ambition to a mattress-thumper like you?

Here, I'll stand up. Take thy knife or thy sharp tongue and strip the skin off me."

"Soft, Will! Soft!"

"Yea, I'm soft. In the brain-sty from ever marrying you."

"Shitter! Oh thou loathsome, high-browed, balding shitter! I know you hate me, that you hold yourself above me, that you think me callous and scheming and no better than dung. I know that, but I know too that thou art a shitter, a rank cow, rancid in your nature, and schoolboyish in your lovemaking. Yea, a priss, and way past saving."

"Better a priss than a sobber."

"Aye, I'll sob, for that's the one relief a woman has from having to wed with jackals, gerbils, and hyenas. I only wanted your kisses, to cover you with my kisses as corn covers a cornfield, as grass covers a meadow. But now you're William Shakeshitter and I'd sooner kiss a hen's crack at high noon in Rother Market."

"Lumpish hag!"

"Sump hole!"

"Witch tit!"

"Lice plucker! Go, then! Go to Londontown, and that busybody Hooker with you. You care more about that fleawort than you do about me or your children. Lie down with pigs, with whores, with rats, with your nasty Queen's Men. Forget your wife and poor snotnose children, forget your warm home here. Nestle your breast up to a rubbishy sonnet, give bum-poke to your Holinshed, let Plutarch whisper in your ears, let Ovid stroke your dwarfish pizzler. Prattle your stage vomit. Oh, go! Expire, shitter, in your own puke! I care nothing what you do, I will be your wife no more. Nay, nor your children your children, either!"

Their controversy put the heat over our yard. It made the very clouds darken and slip lower. Hathaway reared up, snatching her child, murdering Will with her hot stare, with her claws, with her mouth-flood. She kicked him, shook him, turned him, and half-shoved him out of the yard. "Go!" she cried. "There's the road, take it! Tap off! Bale out! Excrete, keck, titubate, and aroint thyself! I want never to see you! You're vile leakings, thick-waisted, fat-necked, big-footed! You're smelly pus that flows like a river! Go! Go!" She foamed at the mouth, threw wet dirt at him, kicked and pummeled, taking pause only now and then to administer quick motherly comfort to the squalling Judith, to say, "Look there, Judith, look there, darling, see that worm? That worm is your no-account, sodding father!"

And Will was spitting his own words back, spewing venom to match venom, flinging his own drippy dirt clods at her; yanking Judith from her arms as each time she yanked the poor squalling toddler back; finally the two of them rolling like demented crabs over the yard, biting, punching, and ever screaming, while I, a pensive Hooker, worried for their mortal safety, thinking to myself, O sainted dog that is in Heaven, where's the dignity, where's the decorum, what tree trunk of poisoned hemlock have these fools eaten? Oh the rotters will kill each other!

But John was running, and Joan from her pottending, and Mary from her wool-binding, and Gilbert with his sleeves flapping, and young Edmund squirt with his bad lungs rattling. They rushed between the love pair, crying "Woe!" "Shame!" "You'll have the law on us!"—then adding their own voices to the melee, taking sides, thumping out allegation and suspicion— themselves now bumping and shoving—so that soon every neighbor was witness and dogs five miles distant were howling and all of Doomsday was ranting its fury through the yard.

And where in this did Hooker stand? I nipped at exposed ankles, tugged at wide skirts; I growled and skipped and tried to keep my paws from being trod on. I whirled and danced, I puffed and spun, and almost enjoyed it. For this was old meat to all of us. It had been going on for nigh on three years, was Will's regular wage whenever he got his courage up and muttered to Anne, to the sky, or to me that London was calling him.

"Next month, darling, after we're wed."

"Next month, sweetheart, after Susanna's born."

"Next month, my liefest one, after I've twinned."

"Next month, dearest, after hog butchering's done."

"Next month, lamb, after woodcutting, after the haying, after the wool's in, once the tanning's done, once the children are married, oh any day, darling, once I'm dead."

I was on Will's side. I too was feverish for London, wanting to think my future was there. Knowing that Stratford was not a dog's town—and if not London, then where? Bristol was Hades; Norwich worse. Birmingham was the curse. Boats made me queasy; crossing oceans was out. Yea, I was moored to Will, but lately I found myself with more than nods for the Hathaway pride as she would entreat him. Dog's a homebody; man, too. She had a right to think she'd wed a normal Two Foot and was wronged to be married to hold pillow in a lonely bed. To have her husband a play-man be, for players are scabrous fellows, lower than fleas. Heart was with him but mind waded toward her. London was scary, London was the plague. Stay, Hooker, stay. Be content with this low life you have. Daring and the hammering verse Will had in him, but I was beginning to see some scent of honor in Anne of Shottery. Some merit in the Hewland harlot, some value in the Hewland butter. For she had fire, and fire, in Stratford, is what was lacking. I regretted and had a bend toward mending my ways with her. In former times, catching her crossing yard or street, bent over with wash or busy at diapering, I had romped to get the straddle and squeeze on her. For she had the juice. Her barn door was ever open and smoking. She jolly reeked with it, biting to my nose and causing my dogger to plop out and hang like a wagon tongue. Squeeze her, I'd say. Get a nose in. Go up on your hind legs and hump her. So right she was to hate me. And to Will's credit that he'd always save her. The prigger would come yowling at her rape screams, driving me off with sticks and brickbats and one day locking me in the store-shed where I all but froze.

Now I'd changed. I had sympathy for her, hearing her each night sweep the sky wide with her prayers, begging: "Let him stay. Let my lover stay and true-love me." And sending Susanna in to sit on his lap, to lay her cheek wet on his: Wouldst thou abandon me, Father? Wouldst thou forsake a poor child? Where is thy love, thy poet's honor, if thou wouldst orphan me? Oh, Father, wilt thou now instruct me in faith and trust, in fidelity and loyalty? Wilt thou speak of vow taking and whereof a vow may be broken? Father? Wilt thou stay my father?

So my Two Foot swam in deep haze, snared between ache and dream. And Hooker his dog swam there too.

The yard cleared. Anne limped indoors, complaining her kneecap was mislocated, complaining of a break in her nose, of hurt ribs and damaged kidney, complaining of loose tooth and cuts so deep she'd be disfigured forever. Saying she'd be black and blue for days, that she'd be better off shut up in the almshouse, never to see friend or foe again. Yet boasting that she'd yanked out great globs of her bastard husband's hair and had got him a good one in the groin as he'd been trying to bite off her ear, and how she hoped she'd crippled the miserable stinker for life. "Let him take *that* up to London!" she pitched out. "Let him know that I'm not his meek kitten, his Snitterfield snit, that he can't walk over me and mine! I'm a Hathaway and proud of it, and I'll not be sniveling toady or footrest to any of you argusome Shacklespeares!"

Will grumbled off, advising old John that he should take Anne Hathaway straightaway up to the rafters and hang her by the neck, and the children with her, if she raised any objection. Saying he was going to Master Aspinall's to look up lines in his Ovid, needing a rhyme to quieten his nerves. Saying he was going to old Higgs, fixer of the town clocks, to have closeup look at the Stratford ticking that was killing him. Saying he was going where it was none of their business. My suspicion was that he meant going the few steps past High Cross to the Bear Tavern, where, with the Swan on the other side, the world first meets Stratford. Or perhaps to the Crown, our third most notable. There to bottom-float his grief under stoups of ale. Or perhaps to find horse that would take him the five or six miles on to dusty Bidford, where he might taunt the nippers with his capacity and spend his night sodden under a crabtree's mantle.

So I togged after him.

He trudged down along the mere, his head struck low into his shoulders as a vulture's. He stood a moment at Market Cross, beating mud from his shoes and rubbing his scalp, soothing a swollen patch on his nose. He cut south down Chapel Street. A Two Foot sinner, moaning his errors, slipped by, dressed in the white sheet of atonement, though Will paid no heed. One of the Ainge lads approached, wanting appreciation for a frog-gigging stick he'd hewn out, but Will slapped the stick aside and trudged on. I hung back, whining a medley of low grievous notes, for he was like to boot me as embrace me when he was in this killing mood. He throwed a rock at the crumbling walls of the house called New Place, and said vitriol to it, though his exact words did not spill up to me. Some chantry priests were out hobbling with spades in their Guild Chapel garden, and Will lifted his ruddy, hazel, steel-raking eyes their way, but did not speak. A wench in Old Town shot her smile at him and wagged a cautious finger: "Want I should massage thy troubles?" she said. "Want I should bliss-rub thee, Mr. William?"

Will humbled on. His pace quickened through the grounds of Trinity Church, and without further tooting, he was at the river. He yanked paper from his pocket, unrolled fine parchment from his breast-shirt, and stood an instant raging. Then he tore his quilled goods up and slung them out over the water. "Stinking words!" he cried. "What's their purpose? Better my verse should sink in Avon's slow oblivion. Better I should sink there myself and make everyone happy!" He leaned, pitched as though to hurl himself in. But the water's depth was meager and it was his own face the pretty surface showed back.

Circling swans daubed at his litter, one or two with squawks to say his food fell short of their liking.

The sky hung low as a widow's bonnet.

How I pitied the bleeder.

I knee-lapped in, all trembling. I tongue-wiped his shoe, whined a snake-wrap around his legs. I lifted my faithful muzzle up to him.

"Begone, Hooker," he moaned. "Better you had followed a maggot to its nursing or turd to its disintegration. Anne's right, you know. My talent's all for humping and wife-throttling and breeze-blowing. I'm sunk down with murderous gloom, all aglow with morbidity. I see premonition, omen, ghosts, the mad flutter of history. Yesterday I thought I'd chase it—rose-cheeked boy flitting with net after green butterfly. So innocent I was. We'll never quit this humbug town. My soul's shriveled. I blush. I flush crimson for what I've let come of myself. Done in by indecision, by brat-planting, by a shrew's meddling. And I'll never tame her. Something is rotten today on this Avon, and it's not these rotten fish heads, either. It's us, Hooker, man on one end and dogger at the other. Over there ewes graze, lambs gambol, the Avon glistens. Yet it's all as ugly to me as Dirty Cawdrey at his slaughtering. I'm a block of shame, a burled knot of protracted hankering. I'm frazzled as a shoe rag, and know nothing. Only that you and I will never quit this rancid town. What's the use? Syllables strung end to end over the flat earth, plays that would singe ears and strangle an audience, what's their value? None. Nothing. The song would still sink in us, for the heart, yours and mine, hangs heavy as an unwashed cadaver. Oh, it stinks, Hooker. Singing's nothing; moaning's the thing. We're all hog-bucketed. Go to, Hooker. Begone. Leave my thoughts to their misery."

His mood had him ringed and I knew he meant it. Knew dog could provide no company. So I slunk away, grim as a pickpocket.

Smoke was churning from Moll Braxton's hovel up the Guild Pit road, wide and blowzy and blackly arrogant. My curiosity was pricked, so I dogged it up the Avon bankside, across the croft past a tribe of goats and a thin harras of ponies, over Butt Close through a drift of swine and a drunkenship of cobblers, through a pace of asses and an incredulity of cuckolds, on over Clopton Bridge to the pits past a chowder of poor people begging me to let me be their supper.

There beyond the pit was news awaiting.

Moll, like Will, was moaning, though with better reason. She lay within a toft of bones and rubbish, bound doubled-over in the witch-grabber's knot, her limbs crossed over, left arm roped to right toes, right arm shackled to left foot. Half-dead, drab as the seasons. Yet her senses were still working: "Dog," she said. "I smell dog." But none understood her, or saw me, as I hunkered down with rat's-eye view behind a rotted, fallen elm. Her miserable shack—worse than the worst dog's doghouse (in that it was not fit for dog) rising out of a damp low cave that a play of twisty roots partly hid—was indeed belching smoke, though it was too rain-soaked for true burning. Mist spread up from the unkempt ground, churning and tumbling. Tree and sky shouldered us, dark as a lid. Imp shapes darted into and out of the surrounding void, cats and other low-life creatures scooted by with forlorn, anguishing cry, and there was a mad trample of Two Feet going one way and another about their loathsome business. To burn Moll Braxton for her weeting (a Latin phrasing), as I gauged it.

"Dip her!" "Strip her!" "Burn her!" was the cry going up from the two or three witch-hunters and the five or ten witch-watchers pacing the section. There was Ralph Cawdrey, of course, and two of the Ainge boys, one down over a root bed barfing up his ale; there was bull-tempered, decrepit Nicholas Lane, swinging a crabtree cudgel; there was a lanky, stewed plowman come all the way from Wootton Wawen; but mostly there were good solid housewifers, the town's go-getters—the old Shriever grandmother, bent and spitting, Crazy Ruth the shearman's wife, and another was the vicar's sister. Cawdrey was driving this last one forth, as proof of Moll's witchery, reputing it that the woman had given birth to a creature half-inhuman. No hands and no feet, with a head blue as a bandanna (he said), though I'd never seen it.

"Is this the witch that commanded it?" hawked out Ralph Cawdrey, up on a stump now, his face red as one of his beef slices. He tugged aloft the woman's arm, half-lifted her off her feet, cracking her elbow as he spun her around to confront Moll Braxton: "Is yonder toe-bound creature the guilty party that bewitched your only-born?" He shook the addled woman, forcing her to look down at the groaning Moll. "Speak, woman," he roared, "else you be a witch yourself!" She gnawed at her dress fringe, babbling some, her eyes flitting about; she nodded to his every word although she understood nothing. "A drink," she sobbed, "a drink, sire, of that what's hidden in your pocket." In truth this stinking bundle of rags knew not where she was; she was out of practice with standing, her head in a fuzz and woolly-minded, as it was out of her custom to stand upright longer than it took to get from ale-sops to ale-sops or puddle to puddle. Cawdrey yanked back her head, twisting, dripping his spittle into her face: "Did yonder hag not appear before you three nights running, in the form first of a cat, then a badger, next a black eel?" The throng rallied. "Say it!" they shouted. "Say it, else you be a witch too." Crazy Ruth was down on her knees packing dirt and twigs into her mouth. Old Shriever was switching Moll about the head. Wind was whipping the black smoke about as though it had it by the tail. The air was rank and cold. Two Feet cut this way and that, stomping and yelling, and more were coming up the road. "Then nod," said Cawdrey, gripping the accuser's hair. "Nod if what the good people here have heard was true. A cat?"

The woman nodded.

"Badger?"

She nodded.

"A black eel that did curl up in your insides?"

"Aye," the woman croaked, digging for the leathern flask in Cawdrey's pocket.

"And was not your child without limbs and motley to behold?"

The woman groaned "Aye" again and swayed, then dropped to the ground, there to cuddle and affix the bottle to her thirsted lips as the throng piled over her to vent their rage at Moll. Terrible, terrible, they uttered, ain't it a sin what witches do! Then to hiss and grapple, spit and chew, trumpet their own allegations forth. Crazy Ruth was hugging her belly, writhing in pain, claiming the witch had bellyached her; Shriever hopped up and down on one foot, vouchsafing the witch had hot-footed her. The Ainge boys were cutting a stake by which they meant to poleaxe Moll and haul her to the pit's stagnant pool. For Moll, they'd determined, was not a black witch that can hurt but not aid, nor a white witch that can do both, but a grey witch whose cozening was all evil.

"She turned salt in my salt box into putrid water!"

"She made my husband upchuck pins!"

"I fed my swine buttermilk, which she changed to urine with a finger!"

"Corn that was green turned to stubble where she walked!"

"A cat died in my house. We shaved our eyebrows, though it did no good."

"She conspired to put snake before my horse, which bolted and plunged us both into the river!"

"She womb-locked Bessie Wigget!"

Moll wept, though it might have seemed she was laughing. Her tongue hung out and drool slobbered from her mouth as she thrashed. She moaned that she wasn't a witch, only a poor, senseless woman born to eke out her living here midst these stones and sticks, one born ugly and crooked in her ways, poor hag with a husband years and years ago who had thought to bury her alive in this cave, then had run off to what future she'd never know. The mob wasn't listening. Stratford wanted purging, they said, from the likes of damnifiable sorcerers with their many fueling teats, their scurvy plundering, their midnight sabbath howling. It was time, they said, Moll Braxton got her honest testing.

"Strip her!"

"Wax her!"

"Burn her!"

Her rags were stripped off, exposing her naked.

"Her teats!" the Shriever hollered. "Count her teats!"

They counted her teats, some three or four they said, though what I saw was normal if a little wizened.

"Throw her trussed up into the pit's festering water! A witch won't sink, which will prove her colors!"

I howled in, biting at Cawdrey's legs as he bent to heist the superannuated bundle upon his shoulder.

"Look, it's her dog," cried an Ainge boy, "though he has the very countenance of Hooker."

I gnawed at Moll's ropes, barking like one bedeviled, my teeth flashing in hideous growl, driving these pea-pickers back. For my gorge had risen. I was fed up with their provincial claptrap, their fin-sucking stewardship, with the full pus and pendulum of their idiotic super-stitions. Better they should think God and the Devil sat side by side in Heaven.

"It *is* Hooker," the Ainge boy said. "The beast has turned demented."

"Aye, the witch has got him."

A few rocks hit me. A boot caught my flanks. Some-one's hands wrung my ears while I chewed on Cawdrey's pulpy fingers.

"Stab him! Stab the dog!"

A hatchet whizzed past my head. Lane with his crab-tree cudgel whacked my brains. Yet I went on boxing. I scattered the defilers right and left. Some were trying to drag Moll away and I sprang, sailed through air, catching wrist between jaws before ever I landed, toe-clawing first one and then another, springing up again and leaping to come down on the back of Ralph Cawdrey, cutting teeth into his neck as he chickened off into brush with me astride him. I thumped off, came snarling back, flung myself between the Shriever's legs, bucked her down, pivoted, and roared at the Ainge boys who dropped their hatchets and turned tail, running fast. I hooked eye up with old Lane, who whimpered and dropped flat. The plowman rushed upon me with whirling stick, but I went through his stick and clapped my best teeth into his throat. He screamed and gurgled down. I swallowed his nasty liquid, took quick lick of blood aflow down my legs, then leaped at another one, rolling with him, clawing and neaping at his soft, pathetic skin. They were flat-footed, awkward, primitive in their movements, with no more scheme to their fighting than a sickened cow, and I wondered why I didn't maim and murder them all. A dark shape flitted by on the road, and in an instant I had it cowering back against a bush, saying, "Not me, Mr. Hooker, I was only taking a stroll." And I smelt his innocence, begged pardon, and let the bugger go. I lunged back, locked four feet atop Cawdrey's stump, snarling out "Where's Moll?" to the space that now was all but cleared, Two Feet tearing off into hillside brush, gut-stomping back down the road, or dragging themselves up to lean against tree and lick their wounds. The earth, in that minute, seemed to beat as though it had a dog's heart, as though dog's heart and earth were one. Yea, the stump's heart a part of it too, for though stump was rotted and cut down to stump's quiet deliberation, chopped to its soil's rot without hope for replenishment, stump was quoting, "Good, good, glad I am to have feet here that's on my side. For as I would gladly give up limb after limb, having ability to sprig anew as the seasons turn, lo they've taken me down to ristly rotted stump as place that throwbacks of the Cawdrey sort might stand on me thumping chest and saying *Burn, burn* to those thats span is different than his own. So good, good, Hooker, good, weigh in and croak the bastards." Yea, dog's heart and earth and rotted stump all beating as one, with none left over for the amateurish, skimpy, arrogant, deluded human thump that is ever turning upon itself itch to itch and peel to peel. Slaughter the bastards, is what I thought. Slaughter them. Drip them in the brine of their own choosing and slaughter them. Strangle the bums. Hack up what's called their spirit, their learning, quest that's said to trod the greater road, and feed what's distilled to a dog's corpse, feed it to essence of stump. Chisel the brutes. Mallet and chisel them. Hack up the Queen, feed her substance to the crows. Show that witch a looking glass. Hack up the Pope, feed his essence to the sows. Nosering the knaves, have them staked on the commons, drive them to market, shear them, butcher them, chisel them, let their flanks hang. Put them in the cockfighting pits, in the bull-baiting rings, and let all stumps, all dogs, clap and wager and dance. It was speechifying I wanted doing, aye, as I tell it, taking no rejoicement at that moment in a canine's abysmal howl. Empty triumph . . . eternal gloating, I won, I won, and all for what? Void, void, I thought, that's all there is. Howl and only more howl comes back, it doomed to die like thunder on a summer plain, with no span of time so meaningfully shallow, so empty, so wretched pure in its silence as that one clapping down after thunder ceases—you won, oh you won, you've scattered the devils, but where's the logic, where's victory's afterglow? Void, void, the true kingdom, void only and no other. Thunder, the firmament closing, then thick rain clunking down, seeping away what little has been won, soaking up howl and heart, pulling it down to the earth's bleeding bedrock and core. Void! Void! So chew them and claw them, chisel them, let them be as chowder for the fields. Why not. For after howl comes nothing, comes bleached bones, then dust's mortification, then petrification, final bitter democracy. So first shove up dog, shove up canine and stump, let them rule this spinning pumpkin-earth, this circling, whimsical ball of slush. Yet . . . Where's Moll? I thought, and said it aloud to stump and my environment. "What's come of Moll as I stand here, yodeling dog, waving my little flag of righteousness? Where's the witch?" And I quickened ear, growled menacingly, spun about, yelped a timid inquiring call. Then heard Crazy Ruth's dumbfuck laughter, glomming on to sight of her bent at the precipice's edge just as she rolled Moll's tethered body off the Guild Pit cliff into the scurvy water sixty feet below.

Kersplash! Kersplunk! Glug and glug—
There went Moll.

And thought, as I went dog-eagled off cliff and out over water to land splat and kersplash myself, how once upon a more innocent and unjaded time, I'd done this before. Dived in, chasing refuse only a jot more noble than Moll. Chasing Will. Saving his Shaker's bones of a stormy, wintry evening when all his lanterns threatened finally and for all time to blinker out. Of how, plunging home from Anne's in the thick of blackest night, having hip-thumped her to hip's content and his legs gone all rubbery, he slipped in a mud hole—"Ant's elbow, Hooker, I'm falling!"—banged his head on stone, and tumbled head-crooked into the Avon's raging current. And went under. Plumb disappeared. Will? Where are you, Will? And me romping a panic's romp along the dark bank, sniffing and grunting and barking a lapdog's feeble growl, keeping apace with the torrent, the river crowed with unkempt black blots and blobs and my Two Foot nowhere in the swirl. Where are you, Will? He was under and perishing, yanked down by fate's tight noose—was gone. Will? I saw a splash of dark hair and whined at it, but it was only log. Say something, you shitter, I barked—dog's omnipotence is limited, you know. No sound, however, only my panic and the crashing water. Fate's noose, I thought, poor Willum, your ass has had it now. But what is fate's reckoning to a dog, when was there ever anything but nasty fate for a dog?—so I snapped tooth at these cold betidings and splashed in. I rowed with all fours and kept my nose crested and thought how, smacked down level with the Avon's roof, in its turbulent tide and swell, I was *with* fate and maybe was myself fate or its mean servant, and my job to alter man's tide, Will's tide, as best I could. I pluggered on. This is a dog's life, I thought, this *is* dog, we are all dogs now—for I heard not a single peep from Will. The rotter was silent for the first time in his life. Now that he needed words, the prisser had none. I tugged against water, skinless as air but in that moment busier, colder, more rank than a bishop's commodious belly. I reconnoitered the moonless path of his fall—and kept heaving. A limb swooshed out of nowhere and cracked my nose; a rock came up and went *plook-plong* against my ear. Death shot past me, crest of waves, tree and bush and squeaking rodents —a thousand foamy shapes. Will? Where are you, roguish singer? Where your verses now? Nothing. Awgg, I thought, the stinker's gone. The stinker's croaked. And me soon with it, worse the rub. My sniffer useless now, my eyes gauzed over with rampaging black, water awash in my head and belly. Then—merciless prank—something tugging at my tail, something heavy as the weight of centuries, yanking and tugging, and I switched back to snap at it, meaning to bite its head off—but saw instead Will's white hand. His pathetic arm holding on. His mouth spitting out water. "Leg's bent, Hooker," he breathed, half-drowned. "Pull me home, old darling."

And I pulled. I verily did. I dogged it, hassling for breath, the centuries adding their weight one by one.

We got nowhere. The river busted us along, two spent chickens caught in a whirlwind.

"It won't play, Hooker," he belched out.

I reminded him hope was eternal in the breast, and more eternal yet when in dog's.

He choked, but held on.

"This is no good, Hooker," he sobbed. "I'm for kings and history, the shoreline's broader sweep. I'm not for this small-fisted, randy, cheapsified sailor's grave. Haul to, Hooker. Pull your daughter home." I plowed for shore, trusting my dog's instinct would know north from south. But dog's womb time, like Two Foot's, has him crouched up like a ball, so instinct is less than one might want of it.

"That way," he spat out. I steered the other course. Black river, black loop of sky, that's all we saw. I snatched glances at him, moaned, paddled, kept my nose beveled up, my ears back—felt my tailbone compacting. Pain ripped up my spine to sting my very nostrils, my eyes blinded from this spitting scribbler's steadfast bulk.

Goodbye to tail, goodbye to dog's one vanity, to his delight in swishing it. Too many chitterlings in you, I told him, oh woe, Shakesfeed, why did you not leave your clack-dish alone?

"I'm finished, Hooker," he cried. "I can't hold on!"

No false dramatizing, I told the rat. I wondered if he wasn't goldbricking me, if the sod's natural laziness wasn't breaking through. My mind drifted; some mean delirium announcing itself. I thought of bone I'd buried once, and grieved I'd never see it. Thought of my old Mam ate up by carrion crows. Thought: They ask too much of dog. His fingers slipped and I twisted back to get teeth on his sleeve; I chomped down, glad to have relief from his tail-pull. "Save me, Hooker," he said, "and I'll never browbeat you again. I'll work and study hard." The rogue swallowed water, went under, came up, saying, "I'll give you my best bed." Oh yes, I thought, when they're at death's door, they sing another tune. I had no faith in it. What's a Two Foot's word? Then we got crushed by another wave, got knocked senseless by a thundering log, got scraped by rock, got sucked under by whirlpool, got sent swirling—came up gagging, belching out water. He was yanking my hair, looping arms around my neck, shoving me down. Clear the rascal valued his own life more than mine. Yet I kept pumping: my legs were twigs in the water, my lungs bursting, my dog's stamina all gone. "Swim, you cur!" he shrieked. "You damnable Hooker!" I hated his words though they restored some little fire in me, wanting more than anything to get the prisser to shore if only to sink

my fangs into his throat and preach to him on dog's
dignity.

We got slung over again. Went under, and momen-
tarily I lost him. Will? I streaked to bottom, found him
snagged by his coat to slimy timber. I brought him up,
his eyes all glassy, his breathing gone. Mine, too, I think,
for I seemed to lose sight of what happened next. But
my toes were touching bottom. I was leaping through
mud, dragging his corpse after me. I got his head up to
a sweep of leaves. I licked mud, fishy odorous stuff, from
his features. Gave kisses to the rascal's cold white face.
I rolled the bugger over and sat a moment whimpering
on his back. What to do? Water trickled from his mouth,
then came out in a pour, as if the whole of the Avon
had been rerouted through him. Already he looked rotted.
He looked seedy and limp, a grey rag. He twitched not
anywhere. "Will?" I said. His eyes stared off unseeing
into the black universe. I whimpered over him. "Will?"
Slurp, slurp. Ahh, Will. It came to me that dog in the
final rule is useless to his master. That dog throws up no
great shadow in the wheel of life. That he's as worthless
as lint behind the door. I honked down for breath as the
trees swayed and winked. Water sloshed in my head. I
could not make my ears stand. My tail drooped to eternal tuck between my legs. Mucus dribbled from my
mouth. My teeth clattered. I shook all over. Wind stirred
up a rustle in the hedgebush and all else. The night's
black wipe buckled; I gagged. My haunches sagged.
"Will?" The river surged by, a lion's roar. A bush was
uprooted where I stood, carrying away a slice of bank
with it. I lugged Will closer in. I licked and pawed. My
very toes seemed shriveled. I stared, squinting, at his
limp legs at jostle in the water. I thought to pray over his

soggy corpse; I even mouthed a word or two, then thought better of it. Surely there was more I could do. I felt giddy and weak, my ribs shuddering, felt my insides wrinkle up. Felt sick. I went down on my knees, coughing up a good mouthful. I heaved. More came. Agg, I thought, dog! So this is dog. I wearied down, my head heavy, my eyelids chugging shut. Thinking, O God, my front paw for a little rest. Yea, rest and sleep and let the curtain spread, let it cover all of us. A tangle of brush flowed up between Will's legs, hung a moment, then swished away. Foam gathered where he lay. Debris snagged on him. I tugged the bloater farther in. Will? I whined at his ear, hopped a mad jig; I dropped down and nestled close to him. Will? I licked his cold fingers; I gnawed at them. Ahh, Will. And it came to me like a star's beam in the nasty unspangled night: dog has legs. Dog can run. Dog can hike up his britches, throw back his head, and run. He can try outpacing death, if that's the need.

So I ran. I ripped off. I zipped through thicket, leapt over log and fence, tore through brambles and streaked over open field. I went at it like a skunker's breeze. And it seemed to me in less time than a star could plummet I was already speeding down Henley, barking my havoc, clawing at the Shakespeares' door. Circling the house like a dozen-footed cyclop's bull, barking out my thunder, doing all I could to wake the dead. For the Two Foot asleep are worse than the dead. They are so slow, so creepy-crawlish, so besodden in their waking, so stumbling and cranky, their brains so fogged you'd think they'd be best off to curl up in caves. Such slugs. Oh, wake up, wake up! I heard clunking and cursing. Heard a foot smack the floor. Now another one. Heard the boards squeak, heard voices raised.

"It's Hooker! I'll kill the humping beast!"

The entire household at last awake, shouting out expletive and threat, thumping out their need for vengeance too. Finally the whole street all the way past High Cross and on down through Wood Street and Rother Market heaving out their hatred of dogs, of mongrels that would bark for every rat that has a sneeze. And some five or six flinging open their doors and bolting through with shoe and stick, scooping down for stones and flinging them. Red-faced and livid in their rage, churning to murder dog. "Hush that cur!" roared out Ralph Cawdrey from his shut-up butcher's place. "Strangle the brute!" And a dozen others raging too.

Old John rushed out to switch me or slit my throat, as Mary—so gentle once her hair went up—leaned at her high window screaming down general pestilence upon dog.

"I'll kill you, Hooker!"

Now all of Henley, all of Stratford, shouting the same. "Kill Hooker! Destroy the cur!" As I climbed up on John, whimpering like a beggar, endeavoring to get my urgent message lodged in his thick skull. Him bellowing out his wrath, kicking at me as his switches stung my hide and broke. While I kept leaping, kept sounding my ragged bark, kept backing up, imploring the fool. Saying, "Follow me, you rat-eyed yeoman's son! Don't you know poor Will's out there drowned like a—" Well, like a dog is what I kept saying.

But what was the use? All these clunkers could think of was hitting dog.

I was beside myself with impatience, wild with fury and badgered by my worry, unable to comprehend their mean thickness and total absence of thought—because by this time Marr knew it and Terry knew it, and a hundred other dogs. Even Wolfsleach was yelping out my rescuer's news. We were all taking their bashing blows, their rain of insults, their lewd abuse. All until the young Edmund squirt wriggled between his father's legs, stayed his hand, and said in his piping way: "Where's Will, my sire? Wasn't Will with Hooker gone over to court that Hathaway slut?" Then something dawning in John, some extra sense freezing his features, scuttling his ranting at dog. "Can't you see, sire?" said the Edmund squirt. "Hooker means you to follow him."

And within a second more, all their cudgels dropped and a hundred footsteps were pounding after mine, as I broke in shortest cut down the street, over wall and dip, through woods and over hill to the Avon's bristling banks. Till finally I again stood panting beside Will's soggy corpse, and they thundered up on us.

John with his knee in the dead boy's back, then hoisting him up to hang by his feet, and me licking the dumb snit's face . . . till the color washed in on his skin and the lips returned red, the scamp sputtering out, "Drowning stinks." Saying, "No honor in that swim." Saying, "Aye, my sire, death's not another coupling I long for." John saying, "Aye, you'll strut and fret your sultry wage another day or two, I think." Next, Will yanking me to his bosom, smoothing down my rump with his soggy strokes, reciting to me and his assembled motley crew: "By my faith, this tail I've pulled has now pulled me. By cracky and by Jove, he's a right royal dog." The gay herring then kissing my snout and hugging me till I almost broke, and having to lay my bones down, dazed by his mushy love and the solid bragging of all.

Later with pudding on the warm hearth and a reed mat to lay my head on, and even woolen coverlet to keep my shivers low.

"He's sweetness, he is," cooed Joan, "and worthy suitor for my hand. Would that I were Four Foot myself, to drop down here by the hearth and give him a maid's warmth."

"*Good* dog, *good* dog," they kept repeating, affirming it till my ears growed up like beanstalks and my eyes swelled up like soup pots and I all but wept tears, harrumphing them like a grinning toad.

A toad, yes, as I tell it, but no more so than that wartbag Moll. " 'Ods pittikins," she wept as I gnawed at her dripping ropes. "God me pity, have I lost my noggin' or have I dropped off to spare Heaven with a smelly dog?"

But I allege my mentality is wetted here; thus I'll retire a spell.

4

The day I first came under my Two Foot's liege was the day two eagles fell from his one crossbow's whump in Arden Wood.

"Fetch them, dog," he'd said, seeing me awatch with my gloaming eye from my hiding place in the high flax field. "Fetch my hunt, you nasty slinkering hound. And if your fangs blood-spot one feathered neck this bow shall next shaft you."

Something in his tuneful commandment stirred ginger in my flanks; I flung off to get him his catch; and fairy-reveled it back to lay warm birds on his fine boots.

"Now there's dog," he said, in grinning wonderment as he gave me pat. "There's a brainish cur who might betoken proper fellowship for my elbows." He looped bird over his shoulders and strode on. At the far tree turning to call: "What's the wait, thou briared ball of dung? Have I not invited thee? Recognize not thy lordly master? Dog my heels home, young whiner, for a man of my trouble needs a long ear if ever he would rake his wits clean. What's your name, docile fleabag? Doth thee like verse? Want some Greek, dog?" *Whap!* "That's Greek for you, lowly cur." And, laughing, again strode on. I followed a shade's length behind, made curious by his loud vulgarity and his purposeful swagger, plus the high way he chunkered rocks into air. "Art thou crabbed?" he asked. "Well, I'm friendly to crab." *Whap!* "That's friendliness for you, you trembling pooch. Hold thy shoulders up, I say. Wouldst thou lick a Two Foot's hand? Hast thou money? Speak up, you harebrained belly-dragger. Where's thy pride? I wouldst call thee Pribble, after him that broke his neck in the river and lay three days unsunken, before the crows pecked him into man's last riddle. You groan? Thou likest not thy name? Then what is it, foul issue of mange?"

"Hooker," I said, breathing it on the quiet.

"Hooker? Nay, *Mister* Hooker, if you be Shake-speare's cur, for although you pant over grass and lift leg at every tall blade, you shall be part gentleman so long as you walk with me. Aye, my boon-mate! My thumb-sucker! But I'd rather have thee, one that calls himself dog, than the company of one who is dog but calls her-self something other. Know you a wench named Hatha-way? Well, she has me holed up with her like lice under chicken wing; she has me licking syrup from her chin. But I'll soon set the wicksy straight. *Odi profanum vulgas*, Hooker—I tell you I loathe the common herd and admit she's first to lead the pack. The juicy rene-gade! Know you any Latin? *Hic, haec, hoak*, she's a jolly-ripe poke . . ."

An obscene, gay, ornately loquacious lad, he struck me, one much given to gibes and rudeness and loose offensive talk. I saw then that I'd one day have to set his brow to more serious thinking on the opposite sex, to gear him right with my woman speech. For although I was myself quick to issue pronouncement on some sillier side of a bitch's nature—such as how when bitch shakes water from herself she does not start with her nose to carry the shake down to her tail but instead starts with tail and proceeds to nose, or how it is she is so prim about her beauty sleep or how she'll insist on wriggling *under* a fence when jumping's the obvious thing—still I knew and would have to teach him that a bitch had more sail to her character than the whole of the sovereign's fleet, plus more backbone on those days when rent was due and no way a dog could pay.

Up the Causey by the borough wood yard, bound for home, I came across the old dog Higgs belonging to the clock tender by that name, who told me Will was still scuttled down at the Trinity grounds holding fast mutter with himself. The Cawdrey gang, he said, was holed up at Swan Tavern, swilling back ale and sack and trying to make sense of some beast ten feet tall that had swirled up out of the guts of a witch on the Guild Pit road and made unprovoked attack on them that had been doing a citizen's job.

"Was my name mentioned?" I asked.

"Aye," he said, "though I put no credence to it."

He held me there for extra duration, wanting to learn whether I knew any remedy for the pendulous scrotum hanging from him. "Give up sweets," I told him, though he found no humor in the suggestion. He then wanted to rattle on about clocks and clock tending and how the job was so vexating to him and Higgs, with no gratitude in it for either of them. Finally, I broke loose and tongue-lapped on, my joints weary with exhaustion. Out of sorts with dog and man. For I'd never encountered witch so heavy, so determined to sink, as was Moll. Nor one so scatterbrained in her logic as I had chugged her roped hide up out of pool. The hag saying *I* was witch, witch or Devil, for who else would bother? Claiming I could have her if I wanted to, though she'd sooner I didn't, for she'd make no pact with one of my kind no matter what powers I promised. A true loony was Moll, and, overall, best forgotten.

A few other dogs of the vermin variety tagged in for sniffs, wanting news or wanting to complain, saying Stratford had got too big to suit their likes, too much always happening, that they'd preferred the town in the old days when a dog could nap under bush for a week and wake up knowing he'd missed nothing no worse than his supper. "It's your kind, Hooker," they said, "that makes all the trouble, always interfering, trying to tell the Two Foot how to run his life, to show him what's good and proper." This was stuff of the ilk I'd heard a thousand times, and I plugged my ears to their harping. They'd say the same of gnats aswarm over their heads and I lacked all patience with the stumps.

I passed the Hathaway on the road, asking where Will was hiding, hunting for him with burning face, but though I pointed first with nose, then with tail, and finally lifted a front foot and issued directions with that, her thickness stayed thick.

"Where?" she said. "Where?"

I slurped her knee a time or two, to show no hard feelings.

"Oh, dumb dog," she said. "Oh, Hooker, you're dumber than him."

But she seemed on the verge of tears, so again I took no offense.

To my surprise, she started walking with me. We

trod along Middle Row, and took the lane by the Crown leading to High Street. She walked stooped over with no bosom to show, staring down but with no notice of where her feet went. A dead crow's company would be more invigorating, I thought.

Though I listened when finally she spoke.

"I did love him and do," she said, "but I can't let him go. I'll lie to keep him here." She patted her stomach, inexplicable to me, looking off sadly into the elms. "Last year he was tying up wreath of rosemary, of nights, and leaving it on my bolster to find. Rosemary and rose, violets and daisy, rue and columbine—oh his pretties reeked the room. I'd be drowsing in bed and he'd enter up on his tiptoes and slide in. Then I'd whisper, 'What are you doing, my Will?' 'Stay drifting a minute more,' he'd say. 'I am only removing your ribbon garters, my dear.' He'd talk like that, so sweet and so strange, I'd all but cry, thanking my lucky stars I'd hooked him. For he knew I had not garter nor stitch of anything else on, only thinking I'd drowse what minute I had till he toe-tipped in. Drowsing's not what he stirs up in me, and never was, though I fear now the juice is waning some in the man. His prick's settling, I mean. Now he's as like to leave dried sticks and briars on my bolster cover, the cretin. One night out of five or six I'm not waked from my drowsing once, which is troublesome to me. A woman gets accustomed to things, Hooker, as I expect you know."

She pulled out a ring from her dress throat and wanly jiggled it in front of me.

"He give this enamel hoop ring to me the night he betrothed himself. I expect you've forgot, though I never will. See how pretty it is, all encrusted with the glitter of lime-pit stones. And this motto writ inside that says—look at it, Hooker!—'With thee forever I'll pace the winding maze.' It's not pithy or clean-tongued, nay, it's no more profounder than a loon's shriek, but he meant it to bespoke his undying love. He meant it to soldier-up his vows. To let me know that while his public face was to lament house and home and rake jest at wife and slander her for her Shottery harlotry—'tis true I did lay down once with Fulke Sandells, but Fulke was all—under our covers and in private, it was affection and honey he packed into my ears, with enough more of it on my tongue and his to sink every barque that floats the Thames. The cretin likes drinking a woman dry, is my opinion of his randy craft. A slug's slime excites another slug, he says. The fool. Oh, he's a fool, no question there, and so lewd he makes my fibers blush. What's to do with him? Well, I'll lie, I will."

She blushed on. Where Sheep Street met Ely we paused. Some pedlar was off in front of the Deege House, carrying on his disgusting trade. He was plucking feathers from a bird he claimed was one part hawk and three parts crow, saying he'd eat it alive for the edge of a single penny, while for twopence he'd swallow it whole.

"It's killing me, Hooker," she said, "keeping him bonny and getting my duties done. I'm all worn down. Up in the morning, pray, smack my face alive, change a diaper, change another. Then clean the house, dress the dishboard, change two babies more, smack my face alive. Then time off to take his squirt between my legs, dress the children, tag after Susanna, cook meals for the household, wash our rags and run off to High Cross for drying. Run home, change the diapers, see that Hamnet's not been eat up by wild hogs, shake the rushes, bake and brew as needed, send corn to the miller. Change a diaper, fetch and carry for John, see to Mary's demands. Cut flowers, cut herbs, pestle and mortar the corn for the babies' gruel, take another of his squirts between my legs, make butter and cheese, give slop to the swine, collect the eggs, change the twins' behinds, et cet and et cet. Oh, I tell you I'm half-dead and run off my feet with wife's work and no time for smoothing Will's moods with kisses that can find route through his trance."

"Yea, work's awful," I agreed.

"Now he means leaving, means quitting his twins and Susanna and me and all in the world who here love him. But I'll lie and cheat to hold him, as it's my Christian duty, you know."

She stopped at the Sadlers' door, where Hamnet was having dialogue with a Two Foot who wanted borrowing money from him. "Twenty-two pigs you have," I heard Hamnet say, "plus four cornfields, three horses, four ox, and thirty-six elms. Yet you want lending from a poor scab like me?"

Hamnet waved, which the Hathaway didn't see, and we peg-legged on. A sheeper came by on his trudging plowhorse. Two chickens over by the Tyler place were having tug-of-war over nothing more important than a wormlike stick.

"Once," she said low, "he was of a mind to say he saw my face in every full moon; and in its slithers, of other evenings, he saw the rest of me. Oh you know he loved me, don't you, dog? But I'll not move from here, or take my children one step to London to die in the plague, as everyone says we would. The plague or starve. For he's no actor, Hooker, as his work with Davy Jones's company at Whitsomtyde clearly showed. Even his doting mother concurs in that. If he goes he'll have his head spiked and a-rot on London Bridge before he's two and twenty—and serve him right for forsaking wife and brats. Yet he's a sodden post, he is. Stubborn, one foot in lead, the other in sunset. Waxing on about how this Stratford sky is a webbed foot eternally pressing him down . . . about how *my* foot is anvil to him. But yea, though he lip-diddles me, I'd perish with him gone. I'd dry up and wither bone to bone. Yes, I'll lie. Will prevaricate my head off, I will."

She stopped, and stopped me, her eyes moistening over as we hunkered in at the Rother Market Cross. Her hands patted, then rubbed her stomach round and around.

"I'm weighted here again, you see. It's another set of twins akick in me. That's what I'll tell him. That will keep him close to home. He'll thunder and rage, he'll make the rafters ring. But he won't leave."

She hoisted her shoulders back, drumbling on.

"It's not fitting to stop at three, Hooker. Three's paltry siring for an Elizabethan man. I know he wants his name to live on, and how else to do it but by planting seed? I'll put teat to his mouth, that'll hold him down. You'll see. When the two of you are old, then you can go."

We turned in at the mere, where I paused to water a tree. She hung by, smiling her watch down.

"Why did you leak there?" she said. "Oh I wish I understood you accursed dogs."

I kept quiet. If I had to give brain to my every act, as she did hers, I'd soon be knitted up like a stew, with life truly insufferable to me.

The wretch was chuckling now.

"You remember how we joked in the olden days?" she said. "How I claimed the finest walk in England was the one from Shottery to Stratford? How he said, nay, the finest stroll was from Stratford to Shottery? How we'd say it, kissing and smacking every inch of the way? How only you, Hooker, knew what else we did? Lo, my spirits have raised, talking to you. I thank you, Hooker."

She dashed off. Up in the yard Terry barked, seeing the Hathaway coming. She was chasing her tail around the tree, a trifler's game. I barked back, but she put her nose up in the air, snubbing me. Hike off, Hooker, is what she was saying. I dropped down in dirt, needing a good belly-rub. A good roll-over. Terry looked cute. I felt some pride in her. She had my long nose and sturdy tail and the same lean haunches that I did. She had the same whitish smear behind the ears. The same slender and elegant bones.

We had good breeding, we did.

We had Mam's old spit on us.

Some barn-sized Two Foot wearing doeskin vest, doeskin britches, leathern belts looping his chest, a hunter's horn hanging from his shoulder, was up by the mud wall conversing with John. I heard him say, "She's not much dog," pointing to Terry; then they stopped and John pointed off another way. "That one's a good sleeper," I heard him say.

Terry pranced over to a newly planted herbal bush and gave it a hard hot piss that steamed.

The Hathaway entered the house, next reappearing with her twinned brats, taking seat on the back-door plank. She drifted off into a dreamy privy-watch of her foaling, swinging a bent sixpence from a cowhide string.

"Gibby-gibby-gee, gibby-gibby-gee, here's crooked six-pence for thee," she sang.

Terry gave the bush another splash. I had never seen her so vixeny before, nor so given to gruff, trollopy noises in the throat. I rubbed my two eyes, moist and gleaky, and got them unglued. My old dogger crept out a pace. Did Terry see? She hiked up her rear. She taunted me with a yelp or two. Wolfsleach had put her in bloom, she was saying, but bloom wasn't all. I watched her locate and paw a bit of rubble out of the ground. She swayed back on all fours, as if menacing rubble to move. Wind caught and fluttered one end, and in the second it fluttered twice Terry made her pounce. She snarled and groped and pulled. Her find held no interest for me. We had each found this treasure a thousand times, and although it was always in a different place and this lent some prideful substance to it, it was as familiar to us as another cockle in the fur. A piece of rag. Some ash cloth dropped by Two Foot, newly scented perhaps, but a rag nevertheless.

A flea crawled up into the corner of my eye, scratched his feet in the moisture there, then shot for the other side. I ripped my face into the earth; when I lifted, flea and half my vision were gone.

Terry chewed on her prize. Dirt fell off and the thing brightened. Marr came out from her sleep and stood poised up on her four legs, attentive, not sure she could let Terry have it, worthless though it was. She inched forward. Terry gave her a snotty, disdainful look. You can't have it, she was saying. Gee-splank off or I'll tie your tubes. She showed Marr her rankish gums and long line of bletchy teeth. She growled low. Yet she was only nose-blowing, as Marr knew. But Marr was out of mood for scuffle and sank back down to lick her knees.

"Piss out of your ort-hole," she told Terry.

I laughed. She'd picked these words up from loath-some Ralph Cawdrey. "Fug off" is what I would have said. But it delighted me to hear Marr giving Terry the rib. We'd been together a long time, old Marr and I, and were as close to having knot-tied as knot ever would be.

I snapped at a buzzing fly. I hate flies. Flies are worse than toads for bringing the dark-house to one's sleep.

I splashed on up the mere and nosed through sedge growing down to the bank. I slithered in for a closer look. John and the Two Foot stranger were down leaning against the pigsty. "Well, we did have another dog," John was saying. "Had two, in fact, but they run away some time back. You know how dogs are."

Ummm. It seemed the stranger didn't. I had yet to hear him speak, and this bothered me. It bothered me the doe-smell his outfit blowed because it wasn't all musky and aged. He had a rich woodsy odor and a for-ester's stance. He had a Regarder's heft. Most, it seemed, he had a way of asking about dog that exceeded routine curiosity about what mattered most in the world.

No mallet, no chisel. No fresh blood on him that I could see. No mention of Lucy or Lucy's arrogant stags, of deer that thinks it can outrun dog by its clever zigzags.

Over by the mud wall a rat overcame his fear and stuck his whiskers from a hole. I leapt up, giving him the close-eye. But no, it wasn't rat, only Devil-Flower fanning in the wind. Marr spotted me and jumped up too. She gave me a snooty stare, then giggled, went down on her back and rolled over, pitching up her legs. With a shameless swish of her tail, she said, "Do what you will with me, Mr. Hooker, I'm not one that can hold a grudge." That's the way it was with Marr; she was always too easy. Whether one was thinking philosophy or searching for lost bone, she was always one to put hind-sight first: the one to plant her legs firm, to hike up her love bonnet, saying, "Do what you will with me, Mr. Hooker, I'm all yours."

Well, I didn't want her. It was Terry giving me the paw-itch, the heart's leak, the angel's drool. She was all doe-eyed lovely in her blooming, and I wanted her. Wanted sister for myself. Who else had the better right? For I was thinking too that the sunset was about to clang down on me, that London was a dream, that my life was tumbling in and soon now I'd tumble with it. My very footpads had an itch and quiver, as though they could feel the chisel's cold tip settling under. And there stood my bloodmate Terry, stirring up all manner of memories pleasant and unpleasant. She was making my dogger yearn to plug up life, to cork up the whole of it so that I might stand back from my tongue-hang and verily ask, What is dog? What is a dog's life? Whereof has he come and whither will he go? Dog is poetic, dog wants a vermin-free muse to spell it all out. So fill up the hole, I thought. Let dogger and hole become one and let time quit. And in the quitting, consider thyself. Uncraven thy blinkers. Stuff the hole! Stuff it, for the hole is a firmament and stuffing it lays quiet the void. Stuff it, I say, as unstuffed thou wouldst ever remain in thy tongue-hang, in thy piddle, whether pyn, poodle, whippet, spaniel, or ditch dog. Plugging takes a dog back to where it was dog began; he becomes first dog. Lay on the rib, says first dog. Lay it on. First dog's howl sweeps down through the ages, unlocks continents, scales mountain, plain, and water. It lays on the covenant. Suckles man. And yet sweeps on, overcoming lion's roar, sheep's bleating, hawk's cry, the gorilla's motley cart-wheeling. Man's mawkish chest-thumping. Dog, the hunter. Dog, the creator. Dog, the rib-layer. Dog, the hearth-warmer. Dog, the great howler. Dog's is the vigil eternal. So sayeth the muse. So blows Hooker.

"Well, we did have such a dog," I heard old John telling the stranger. "About so high. About so long. With a whitish smear behind the ear, just as you say. Aye, and Hooker was that cur's name. But where that dog has got to I couldn't say. Probably dead, if you ask me, because that dog had a fixation for cart wheels. Cart wheels and horse hooves, he couldn't keep away from them. Yes, he'd be kicked to death by now, or run over, because that's the kind of dog he was. A nuisance."

I was remembering Mam. Old Mam, my mother. Remembering the batch of us squirming over each other to get the suck on Mam's warm teats. We were off gypsy in the bush in those days, one rung up from sodden mulch, two rungs up from rubble or scrub rat. Hardly what you'd call a proper dog. Lice meat, leaf mold, a brainless rubbishy litter. And old Mam not much better. Poor bush-curs we were, with no past and no future. We had twelve in Mam's birth heave, and naught but skull bones and dirt to cleave to. Times were hard; they were all but whining impossible. Daily our numbers dwindled. Twelve became six, six became two—myself and Terry. Not to say Mam didn't have pride, that she didn't have eye glitter; the survival of two, as she told it, was double the usual. That was civilization for you, Mam

said, and what came from being of plucky stock. What
happened to the rest? I sometimes wonder. In the day
Mam was out hunting our clack-stake, pup lived by his
own trailblazing. Several wagged off into nettle and
vine; a ferret got one, Mam got others. A rat pack got
the runt, and would have got me if they'd been looking.
But ratpacks lack the deft sniffer; they lack the patience.
What they really lack is an astute leader. Mam was forever fretting that her teats would go dry, that her milk
would run crooked. When the meat hunt went poorly,
we were what she looked to for sustenance. Once of a
cold moon I saw her swallow my brother Dopey, though
at the time I didn't quite clepe to what she was doing.
I went on teat-pugging. Dopey was up in her jaws, then
I felt a great teat-rumble, and Dopey wasn't there any-
more. It was only when my own head hit Mam's mouth
that I started squalling. I kicked and wriggled toward
the moon's flash, saying, "Mam, my Mam, what are you
doing?" Mam appreciated that. She spat me out, saying
I had the gaption. I had the gaption and I had the
dogger. She licked my fur, slick as skunk sweat. She
talked to me. She threw her paw over me and began
preaching: "I've been a busher too long," she said, "to
change my ways now. I like it wild. But wild ain't easy,
Hooker. Wild is scab-foot hard. Wild gets you neurotic
after a while. So what I'd recommend is the Two Foot's
world. Two Foot will kick you, he'll burden you with
how hard *his* life is, but at least you have a fighting
chance with him. He *may* keep your clack-dish full. He
may give you a scratch on the head now and then and
a kind word. It's unlikely, but still he may. Two Foots are
strange, they can be bleeding disgusting, but they seem
to like us, God knows why. You've got the dogger. That

gives you the edge. Take care of Terry. She'll bloom her-self one day, and when she does I'd like to think her pups were dry and warm. I'd like to think too that you'll always remember where it is you come from. That you'll always wage battle for the underdog and not go high-hat on me."

Mam had spit, she had backbone. I tell you, that dog had real sand. "You will rise up," she told us. "You will. You will shake off this bush mud and wear proud fur. You will not always be the fleabag your Mam is." Thus spake Mam. "Promise me. Promise me you will."

I was bigger and had the dogger, but Terry was clearly Mam's favorite. Me she was forever picking up by the nape hair and whirling off into briar and thicket, but Terry she was forever love-licking. "A bitch will show she's bitch by how her fur gleams," said Mam. "Your opposite just shows dogger. And though they think it is, though everyone thinks it is, let me tell you that dogger is nothing special." Terry got the best teat, the warmest snug, Mam's most gentle paw. She got all the secret whispers in her ear, and all the secret looks. And she was first to get the meat once our weaning came.

Not that meat came often. And less often yet, once Mam went away for good. "Where's Mam? Oh where's our Mam?" So we whined through many a long moon, Terry and I, snuggling together for mercy's want and trembling for each shadow that moved. "Save us, Mam!" we'd screech. "Oh come back, Mam! Oh why have you left us, Mam! Mam! Mam! Mam!"

Some as vouched they'd seen a dog of her description down Wincot way. Wilmcote? Which Wincot? Our speaker wasn't sure. Another said she was running with a mad pack in the forest green near Hillborough. Between the Milcotes, some said. In the river, one trash-mongrel testified. Done in by cart wheel. Running with a short hair. Run through by a crossbow during the hunt at Hampton Lucy, still another rumored. I learned in time not to ask, for the answer put Terry in a stupor. "Oh, where's Mam?" she'd sob. "Oh, I miss our dear old Mam."

One wet snarly brutal day we were tailing after crippled bird and saw in a ditch what looked like Mam. The pile had her fur. It had what was left of her nose.

"Is that Mam?" asked Terry. She haunched down to whimper whilst I made the vultures spin.

"Is that Mam?"

Well, it had her tail. It had her knees. The eyes had been plucked out, but the sockets had Mam's laconic way of seeing things.

"Oh, Mam! Oh, Hooker, it's our Mam!"

She tried scratching gravel over the picked bones. She railed at the floating death birds. She pawed and spat at the flies. She moaned and crooned and vowed she'd never leave Mam's side.

"No," I said. "No, that's not Mam. That's not a whisper of our old Mam. Mam's coat was thicker and darker, and you can see here how this one lacks Mam's longer bones."

"Are you assured, Hooker? Have you the certainty that this isn't our loving Mam?"

"The skull's all bent. The nose is shorter. These teeth don't have Mam's old bite. No, Terry, this isn't our Mam."

So she was convinced, and eventually we got back to

chasing bird. We even caught one. And I let Terry have it.

"It's tender and juicy," said Terry. "I wish Mam could be here to taste this."

"Mam's got dozens of birds, Terry. She's got a whole tableful. No, this minute our Mam is probably eating shank of cow, probably licking her chops and thinking of us."

"I hope so, Hooker. She was a good Mam. She was the best Mam in the whole wide world."

No. No, that hawker's supper by the roadside wasn't our Mam.

But that night and for a league of nights thereafter I went back myself to moan and croon over those dead bones. For it could have been Mam. It might have been Mam. The rot was fierce but through it all I smelt something familiar. Some lingering scent that bore up tidings of Mam's specialty.

Mam—or poor nameless dog? This is what nose told me. A single Two Foot, wearing worn cowhide, had dragged the carcass into ditch. His earth pats had a rye scent, and his boots a sheep smell. Had his coupewaine hit Mam as she yapped at the slow wheels? The cart had been pulled by an aged, clopping mare with one loose shoe. They had limped on down the road to a sod-packed hovel in the sink at Snitterfield. From my peep's knoll in the brush I saw the very cart and mare, and even the Two Foot who had ditch-dragged her. But I didn't believe the Two Foot I saw had deliberately earsplit Mam. Or even that he had been involved. No, his was a Samaritan's act, removing Mam from the road. For he owned two friskers of a low and cockered size whose tails wagged when he called. And it was what they told me: that their master dearly loved dog. That the carcass had been long in the road when they had happened by.

"Where have you been, Hooker?" Terry asked me. "I heard you howling. Were you howling for Mam?"

Aye. Aye and goddamn. A dog howls for his Mam. His howl cuts across mountain, sweeps across land—and if he's lucky and the wind steers it right, then howl comes rumbling back, saying "Here I am . . . here I am and always will be . . . your lost Mam."

Lost, yes, and nothing to succor the soul but a grieving ghost. From that time on, for Terry's sake, I demeanored myself to meet all peril and take the jaw-measure of all foes. We lived from moon to moon and rib to rib, assaying cautious path over the uneared ground, hiding away in brush and stagtail swamp until jaw and muscle growed. Bateless in our hunger as the tick was in his, we did the sneak on deserted thatchtop, barn, and pigeoncote, ate bugs and weech, ate the mossy bark of trees, chawed at log vermin and field rat, pounced on lamed hare and burrowing mole—went after the foysened cluckers when their heads were under wing and Two Foot's clunking boot was prone.

Aye, Mam, we growed. But never was our promise kept to shake off mud and rise up. And now it seemed to me it never would be. Our bones too would be bleached by the roadside, slung aside like filth in the way of traffic better than us.

"Well, you *say* he killed deer," John was telling the stranger, heading him up to street. "But I say where's proof? I say what matter it to Lucy that he have one deer more or less. I'd remind you and Lucy that I was once bailiff of this town—bailiff and alderman and constable and ale taster, too—that I've been everything in this town a man can be, and I tell you we don't take lightly riffraff notions about expeditating dog. So you can take your chisels and go."

"Hooker's the villain," the man said. "You have him here in the morning. Our cutting's simple. It won't hurt much."

"Hooker," said John gravely, rubbing his chin. "Nope, no dog here by that name. Must have been some Shottery dog. Everything runs wild up there."

In the street the stranger put finger to John's chest. "See that the cur's here," he said. "And the lad that owns him too."

Marr ran up, jumping down into the stream with me. She splashed, chased a minnow or two, then brought her head beside mine. Together we watched the stranger pass down Henley. Another man joined him, then another, then all three turned in at the Angel.

"Who was he?" she asked.

"Black Shag," I said.

A bee or wasp zipped by, and Marr took off after it.

I lapped a few drinks and stood mindlessly swishing my tail. I studied my feet in the churning water. I wondered what it would be like to have none. I wondered if Will would hitch a crutch to my leg so I could walk with him. Wondered what it would be like growing old and useless in Stratford. Whether I'd end up like that dog Higgs, dragging my scrotum wherever I went. Hobbling off on my elbows into dismal eternity. Into rot. Dog dust. Chemicals of canine.

Oh, boo-hoo.

I looked down at the stones in the mere, and it seemed old Mam's face was looking back. She had a scowl on and moss growing out of her nose and a hay-thrasher's dull longing to be elsewhere. "That's right, Hooker," she said. "I'm dead and gone and you owe me nothing. You owe no one nothing, least of all yourself. What's life, anyway, but a hill of beans? Don't feel bad. I never expected nothing. To tell the truth, I was not much myself. I might have been among that Two Foot rabble trudging poverty road, but instead I was dog. And no good, like everyone said."

I whined, put my foot over the talking stone, strapped paw over my eyes. Felt my own tears leak down.

Sob, sob. (Blub, blub.)

I remembered once, talking with Will and him saying dogs were lower than the low, I'd pointed out even Aristotle had noted favorably the link between dog and man: how each shed his teeth similarly and had a single stomach that daily required replenishment. "Who?" he'd said—and taken out his pen to write it down. "Aristotle who? What's he done?"

Remembering how one time I'd been running in Arden Wood and had flushed quail—and how the minute I leapt and caught the bird in my mouth, another dog leapt and snatched it too, and how we came down rolling and scraping, each claiming the catch was his own. How, midst our arguing, the quail scooted away. He was about my size, that dog, though meaner and heavier, and after he'd whipped me he stayed on to converse a while. "I see you're a loner," he said, "like me. I see you live by your wit and claw, how you're the kind that lets nothing tie you down. Ah, you remind me of someone," he said. "Give me a minute and I'll come up with the name." He strode around me, sniffing and studying, a most inquisitive cur. Finally he let out a long loose growl. "I've got it," he said. "You must be the son of, or related to, a bitch I knew once over at Kenilworth when I was fighting bear. Just a pup I was, that time the Queen came down to Leicester's castle for one of his fine fetes. The Princely Pleasures, they were called, though if you've ever fought bear you'd have another name for what went on. But, yep, I knew your mother. Knew her well. A fine hump of a dog. Come to think of it, you might even be my offspring."

And he told me about Mam in her youthful days. How the Queen had stayed three weeks, then gone away in a huff, but before she'd gone how there'd been bull-baiting one day and bear-baiting another—and a hundred dogs dead. "It was one night, crawling up in our kennel to lick wounds and die, that I found myself licking what would have been your Mam. And, oh Hooker, what a bitch she was! How she'd make that bear's fur fly. And mine, too, once I'd tackled her."

We'd had a friendly romp then, him and me: father and son. Maybe.

I sighted Will over by the lime trees at Trinity Church, hunched up next to stone. HERE LIES and HERE LIES and more HERE LIES than ignorant beast can count. I knew the spot as Shagspere's graves-place, for there, flat down, stretched the two sisters never seen by him. Margaret, it would be, and the earlier Joan. Trumbled off to black sleep inside their first year. Plus Ann, la-mented seven-year-old. Plus hundreds more brittle and fleshless under the kempered ground. *Hic incepit pestis,* as the scribe was bound to script down. Here begins the plague. Here ends heart's leak and lung's shroud, leg rot and brain stew, consumption's fit and drunkard's breath and hunger's last gnaw. Here ends it all. Now we lay you down.

But not dog. Dog's physician does not describe a cause for dog's departure, other than to say, "This one was kicked to death and that one starved, this one was hit by cart wheel and that one mourned away for lack of a master's love." Nay, dog's curse comes announced by wind and wind says, "The maggots shall eat you all. One way or another maggot shall rule the world." Dog is loose in the memory or he'd rise up and demand a higher shelf for his life and invent sweet myths to explain it all. Once upon a time, two ticks in the Garden, one saying to the other, What this place needs is a dog. . . .

In London, I've heard, in the plague year when a thousand each week die, the Two Footers overflow the ale rooms and carry their revelry into the streets. They drink and whore and give the thumb-nose to death. "Come and get me if you must," they sing, "but I'll not gnaw my hands in prayer or sit here trembling in the wait of thee." In London when summer heat gives the plague its run, men in packs hunt down dogs to club them to death. Thinking dog is the plague's cause. Thinking it's dog that squats it down. Idiotic. They'd do better to be beating their sticks against those who give the order to them. Yea, dog is nothing. Dog is to be wiped out. Dog is four-legged and tailed and God knows what it will not eat. Drive up a red cross over the pit that holds them. Throw another dead dog in. To halt plague, make steady use of wormwood and rue; use purges, powders, perfumes. Wash down your entries and doors. Throw another dead dog in. Smear on frog's spawn, goose dung, pudding made from cat's brain. Hang up a bride's virginal hair. Widen your pit and throw another dead dog in. So our law gives out. So our bailiff says. Yet dog knells what his master does not: that the pestilence had its start in Asia where the rat had his; that the rat went shipboard and brought it here; that the flea sucks infected rat, then sucks man. London, I've heard, is aswarm with rat. Call up Hooker. He can do a dog's work there.

Such was my thought as I watched Will pick flower from grass. His mother had brought sweet herb and put it over Joan's deep head. Her firstborn, a shaky start. The herbs were past flowering, into seedlings now, and my Two Foot plucked them. He scattered seed to air. "I as lief would die with milder mercy on my brow," he murmured. "I as lief would ring it out that death may have its peace, its honeyed coffers, its heathery Hereafter, though for my pennyworth there is a fairer sleep. What say you, Hooker? What say you to foul death?"

I said nothing. Will, I knew, did not wish that I should. He was only spitting his gall out. "Thou, too," he whispered. "Thou, too, friend Hooker. Bound we are to mummify our bones here."

Not mine, I thought. Mine will be carried for luck in the Regarder's pocket.

Will strode on past his own blood's plot, raising boot to other stones most niggardly and leaning.

"Faith, Hooker," he said, "here molds the grave of our old miller, Roger Greene. I kick the stone but think not that his soul will turn over. Not in his death with near the count it did while he lived. Come kick the stone, Hooker. If you can't kick, then piss on it, for that's all our breathing's worth."

But I wouldn't.

Will sighed low. "You see here four of his that were buried that very same year your liege first snouted light. Why was my own baby's cooing not sopped out? One in seven in our simmering backwater met their reaper in the year I was born. Aye, I know, I was with Snitterfield relatives lapping up goat fat. Lapping up clean air, and thus survived. But for what, Hooker?"

He strode on. "And here lie the bones of two sons and a daughter of Richard Symonds and his simpering wife. Yet Richard may still smile and his ladyship still simper. Would a Hooker hook that natural?"

And strode on, kicking earth and stone, his words rushing as he got the lift of things: "Here lies Richard Perrott, and here his wife. The grass grows taller over her, Hooker, why is that? Here between them their son and four daughters, a full family stamped out. All gone in the year of my issue, 1564. I am twenty-one years green, Hooker, and nothing. When Hathaway calls me wart, calls me warthog, calls me unweeting slops, the tough oak has my mark right. I'm as tied up here as her sabbath bonnet. I'm as pinched in my universe as her flesh is girdled. They'd have a ring in my pig's nose, my brain as much shut up as pigeons in a pigeon house. But I'll not have it, Hooker. I'll run. I'll weigh my legs against the London road. Someday," he muttered. And stomped on.

"Down here, Hooker, three more. And over there, Oliver Gunne, apprentice to the weaver. And beyond him, another who was weaver but who is himself now unwoven. How long, Hooker? How long in the ground ere a body rot, when it went to earth ripe with unused ginger and the countenance still dewed? What counts a life, smelly dog, thou impervious mongrel, ugly night barker? What is to count mine? Three barks? Two? A playful growl? Contented whine? . . . Should God think to scratch between my ears as I here scratch between yours? What is my measurement as a dog-face would reckon it? Should we call in the diggers now? Would you have me hike up my leg as you hike yours, to make no more than piddle against these humble stones? Is that a Shakespeare's worth? . . .

"I tell you, Hooker, this Stratford—Anne and Susanna and my beauteous twins, though I love them—it sits like a gnat on my tongue. Thou shouldst swallow, says Anne. Says my mother, says John. Being stalwart to them's no more than accepting whatever poultice wind blows. . . .

"I would piddle, though not on Stratford's stones. My piddle would arch elsewhere. Shakespeare's not a mourner to be satisfied with sniffing at life's unfilled bowl. And I sniff it here. Sniffing verily packs me in."

I stared bleakly off at the paddling, humdrum swans, getting the taste of something rotten in my mouth. Feeling out of patience with Will and half-thinking here mouths off a weak-sponged fool. A sniveler, all bellyache and drivel, no hum to his cross-eared tune. Thinking his words had become too familiar, that he was finding false harbor in them, that it was all vile excrement, malodorous, encrusted, wormy. That Anne was right: he'd prefer to confess a felony than get down to hard work.

"Cat shit," I groaned. "Cat's piss and bird's dribble. That's rubbish, Will. Buggery's hard too, but still it's done."

He hard-eyed me, taken aback, rankled that I would add my drop of spite to his malefic mood.

Let them chop *you* off at the knees, I thought to
myself. What's the loss?

The day had turned colder than cool. The sky was
dark and yeasting.

"It's low," he laughed, unaccountably, "though it
does not reduce me."

We paused to take study of the cucking stool by the
river farther on, where Hathaway, he affirmed, ought to
have her haunches damped for scolding him—and looked
beyond that to the creaking windmill. "As chitterling
makes good pudding," he sighed, "so would my life's
churn be as fair as that."

And mine, I thought, hobbling on peg legs.

A pack of roguish boys were at game in Avon's
marsh, and we took the knell of them. Some frogs they
had, and log and plank, and plank laid across log, and a
stick for bashing frog as the plank was struck and frog
tumbled into air. "There," grumbled Will, "was I once
the same as them, a twerp with more load in his britches
than was carried in his head. Ah, it's a swinish age.
Though I am not one to rail against it; only one to tell
it as it's so."

Aye, I thought, and that's why your sight has no
more worth than a blind man's bow.

He signaled *hush*—"Hush, Hooker!"—and swept his
body low, copting ear to ground. "Listen," he whispered.
"Do you here, as I do, Charlotte's anguished cry?" Even
the mawking boys stilled their frog-bashing to lend ear
our way. For Charlotte's cry was ever over the graveyard
to crinkle skin and run the shudders along the spine. To
make hair stand on end. "There's money in this," said
Will, "can I carp it right," and, his eyes enlarged, he

went rapt, intensifying my sense of the thing: Charlotte Clopton, in the year of Will's birth, with golden hair and eyes of blue, had been plague-stricken and called dead and rushed away to burial in the crypt beneath Trinity Church. In seven days another Clopton succumbed, and again the mourners sobbed off to holy ground. Tomb was opened and there, on the high stone steps, with mice-chewed face, was Charlotte in her grave clothes clawing at the door—not dead by plague but buried alive. So her cry was perpetual now: at still twilight her pawbed scratchings, her doomed wail, echoed beyond the crypt door; of black Stratford nights her white bones swept through lane and street, they rattled doors and hugged windows and came screeching down chimneys, looking to leave their mark of death at every house. "You underestimate the clankings of history," Will told me. "There's much to be said for looting the past."

Way up on the Lime Close some demented boy was pitching a black cat up high into air, and catching the creature as it came wriggling down. Then pitching it up again.

We stalked on. The same Old Town whore who earlier had corked her finger at him now hipped encouragement once more. Passing, Will tickled her chin. "A penny, sire," she said.

"Hast thou greased thy legs?" he asked her.

"No, sire, but thou may, if thou wished, lick them smooth."

"And my dog, may he lick too?"

"Oh, sire, Hooker's licked my hands a thousand times."

"But not your feet?"

"Aye, and all over, for he's a randy dog. My ache is that he cannot pay."

"You'll get paid," Will said, "at high noon on the whipping post."

Her gales of laughter pursued us. "Nay," she called, "but I shall let you birch me. A penny? One penny?"

Will laughed too. "Everyone is for my money," he jibed. "They are for the purse I shall have one day. For a penny I could stop the night at an inn and catch good sleep. Waste not, Hooker. Hold back tithe. Keep your coins stitched up in your frock as the bishop does his." At New Place he paused to speak more. New Place was old now. The brick and timbered dwelling had possessed a mighty face once. Now its visage weighed more with rat and the mischief of run-about boys. It was decayed and crumbling and unlived in. Yet in my Two Foot's sight it still hung high as the moon. "There you see it, Hooker, Hugh Clopton's old manse. What you see is cobwebbed rot, is spider's crawl, but what I see is the house I shall have one day. It is Stratford's great house, fit to have the Shakespeare crest bedecking its door. It has ten fireplaces, Hooker, and more rooms than Hathaway has brains in her head or bunions on her Shottery feet." He beamed, seeing New Place his. "Underhill's a rogue, but he's skimpy and I can get it cheap. Susanna shall grow up there. Her suitors shall call on me and I shall give them fast cheek. I will have her marrying nothing less than a lord. My twins shall scribble their learning on these walls. Queen E. shall stop over, as she did at Leicester's when I was a modest, giggling boy. She called the Earl her Sweet Robin then. I shall be her Sweet William. Oh a clown can make her laugh, but it will take Sweet William to keep curl in her hair. Stick with me, Hooker, and we'll go visiting her. I'll take you inside her Great Hall and behind it into the Great Chamber, and from it into the Presence Chamber, and if you don't piddle the tiles I'll take you into her Privy Chamber where you can plunge your nose between her great white thighs—if, that is, there's room for us both. Anne says it's whores I want, but I tell you it's the Queen herself I'd thump down. Am I vain, old Hook? Do I prance? Bite me, fine cur, and bring me back to raw earth."

He whooped laughter, slogging on.

His mood shift, his boasting, was enigma to me. Dog wants only a dry hole. Wants only tasty bone. Wants the cockles off him. All else is luxury.

Yet dog I knew had made contribution to the affairs of men. St. Hubert, for instance, converted to Christianity one day by sighting of the head of Jesus riding between antlers of a stag shot from cover by a roving mongrel.

I hated the cocker for making me grin.

"I know," he said, "man swirls up out of dust, Hooker, but where does dog come from? From wolf? Fox? From hog swill?"

Rubbish, I told him. Dog is a species separate from them. All dogs come from first dog, old Howel the Good.

Will chuckled. He dropped down to all fours and gave a howl himself. "That's rich, Hooker," he said. "Next you'll be telling me I'm kin to wild turkey or that the Hathaway has feet meant to wear shoes."

Cat will mew, I thought, and dog will have his day.

We plugged on, past a gang of surly bowlers headed for the Guild garden.

A poulterer was scalding chicken, and the chicken flipped from her hands to flop broke-necked into the street. Nothing stood between my greed and hers, but I let her have the flapper.

A pinch-faced rickety boy, said to carry the pride of decrepit old John Wheeler's illicit blood, threw a stone at me. Then disappeared, bug-eyed, behind his mare's loose skirt.

The sergeant-at-the-mace William Rogers clattered by in a suit of light yellow leather and five-shilling boots, shaking his rod at a careening drunkard.

I stopped short, sighting the Angel ahead. Visualizing Black Shag and his Regarders inside it waiting for Hooker. Will tripped over me and went down in a sprawl. "Oh, you crapper, Hooker," he shouted. "Can a stinking dog never learn how to walk?" He'd banged his knee and, to take the pain from that, he drew back and swatted me. "Mange!" he said.

I backed up. I thought I made out Black Shag at the Angel door, picking his teeth with a chisel. A siege of trembles overtook me. Pure livid cowardice. I was so unaccustomed to the feeling I almost sobbed. I almost melted down into a putrid pile.

"Buck up," said Shake. "I didn't hurt you that much."

"They mean to cozzen me, Will!" I screeched at him.

But he didn't hear me.

"Oxford's the shorter route," I yelled. "Let's take that! Let's take it now!"

He didn't hear. One of the Quiney crowd had honked his name and they were slapping shoulders, hugging and kissing each other. Being bleeding disgusting. "I'm thirsty," said Will. "Let's drop anchor." Together they struck a quick pace, leaning toward Swan Tavern. So much for his penny. So much for dog's company.

An insipid supercilious insensitive puke.

Three birds were twittering in a high tree.

The sky was edging down.

A tannery wretch washing her door sloshed her hot lye at me. "Away, cur!" she said. I bent knee, slithering on.

A Clopton two-wheeler clattered over the bridge, in it, riding stiff-backed, a Clopton lady with a tame bird swooshing bright feather on her arm. Then was gone.

A load of young pole-wood was pulled by, bound for the salt-boilers.

A dog pack was yowling out above the Guild road beyond the gravel pits.

A ragboy came out from a gate, put finger to snotty nose, and blew. Then, bewitched and brainless, stood sharp enough to know—like me—his life was leading him nowhere. A wild, scab-cheeked girl thin as a twig did pirouette outside her door, laughing shrill when her mother broke out to shake her and lead her roughly in by the plat-tail.

At another door, near High Cross, a spread of patchy mud-hide had slumped down. Then its mud-hat lifted and, above motley beard, red eyes blinked. "Is it boar?" this Two Foot croaked out. "Wild boar? Or is it dog? Come give a lick, friendly beast." The sack had black teeth and generous stench. Ruffians more advanced in the line had met their fists' pleasure with him. Yet he was gloaming and sunny, a mirth-grabber, for he was flat-faced drunk. "Give a lick." He grinned. "Fetch over, and I'll lick you." I held back. Why? Dog likes licking and is no temperance officer. It is this licking, plus his mindless romping, his drooling and tongue-lapping, his endless yapping, that has kept him to four legs rather than two. But the ape stood and look where it got him. What then was there to look for, hope for, attain to? Perhaps I held myself too good for this ale-soaker. Perhaps I already saw myself in London, mascot to the Queen's Men, saw myself at court kneeling before Big Red the Queen, saying, "Aye, I'm Will the player's dog." A dog could. Hooker could. I visioned myself sleeping on a soft pillow, running with hoi polloi. Wearing neck lace, puffed sleeves, a russet wig, my dogger fitted with a jeweled case. "Now there gaits a nobleman's dog," people would say. "Keep your sticks off him." I could prove myself serviceable too; I could station myself at the theater door, baring my teeth in the fright of horse thieves. I could run through the streets in loud bark, announcing, "The play is on, the play is on: *The Tragedy of Hooker*, in three full acts, by Wm. Shakespeare, hark ye, hark ye, hark ye! See how Hooker, prince of dogs and Lord of Mange, got his limbs chopped off! . . . See how the mighty mongrel bled and died!"

Watch for the red flag.

Yea, throw another dead dog in.

The swigger before me was trying to stand. He cackled a merry cackle, or something with the resemblance of one. His fist gave the throttle to loose tooth and fingers came out bloody. "You're that cocky versifier's pooch," he sneered. "Him that was blown from the nest before he could peep." This was what Will wanted away from—he was known here; his way was furrowed, his horizon fixed. He required new ceiling, relief from familiarity's contempt. A broader sky where the pen was honored, where the name Shakespeare ceded nothing.

To be not Will the glover's son but simple Will, a player.

Dog, too. "See Hooker rout the Danes, see him drive Frenchmen away from the church door!" Hooker's gone, where went Hooker? "Oh Hooker's to London, to start over."

But cripple couldn't go, nor would Will, without me to make him pick up heel.

The drunkard Two Foot crawled his roped hair nearer. He was gap-toothed and hideous in his grin, like some bag of bilish wonderment rolled down from a cave. "A lick, one lick?" he said. His slobber eked down his gristled chin to stretch in goopy puddle over his beard. "Won't even a dog kiss me? Wild boar will. My wench will. Go and fetch my old hag, son?" His arms lifted. His bloated, coal-bag face was one vast smile. His lips puckered. He closed his eyes, waved his arms. He wanted to pelt the entire world, it seemed, with his great kisses and hugs. "One kiss, son? Only one?"

I darted in and gave him his kiss.

His arms closed on me before I could run. He caught my paws and lifted my front legs up. And as this happened, something of his old filth seemed to shed off him. His eyes, next to mine, had nice sparkle in them. Some firmness he had in his chest. He was not all ale-sops. Not all lice and bugs and reeking slops. He leaned back, holding me erect. He grinned his fumes into my face. "They say you're Hooker the dog," he said, "servant to the high-pocked snit. But I say, with a little practice, you could stand up. Walk on your hind legs, dog. Do it for one minute and I'll never touch licker again."

He let go and—funny thing was—I found I could. I walked with no strain to the left, then to the right, then over a muckhill, then took the same ground back again. It felt curious and, all in all, kind of grand: it put a ripple in my ears, a tingle in my spine, but I knew not what to do with my tail. It was agreeable and easy—nothing to it. But I saw no point in it; it didn't measure up to a dog's eye gaze. I dropped back down.

The Two Foot nodded and beamed. "Aye, Hooker," he said, "and I knew you could and thank you for obliging. And as I'm a drunkard good to my word, I'm now home to my hovel to bed-in with wife and child, never to drink again, my son."

A witchified man, loony to call a dog "son."

The young Edmund squirt darted by, flinging his way home. "Look up, look out!" he cried. "The black crow flies! It flies low and will sweep you up!"

It was only sky this squirt meant, and sky was flying nowhere. It was only sinking down to give invite to Stratford's demony sleep.

The Avon's croakers were beginning to croak.

Two Foot's life was beginning to hunker down.

The corn market was wrapping up. Ralph Cawdrey was out in front of his stall, salting lamb, shouting meanness at widow Baker, the hunchback, whose job it was to sweep and shovel the market clean.

Raven, the bridge cleaner, was on his way.

The dogs above the pits were still running, some twelve, I think.

Up there Moll Braxton would be stirring her pots.

Candlelight showed in the window of the Sadler house where Will and the Hathaway were like to come for fun.

The constable poked his strange rounds, wary for unmuzzled dogs.

We'd never leave. I'd become Stumpy the knock-kneed cur and Will would take his place beside oxen, pulling a plow.

Some eight hundred feet down the Warwick road a hank of vagabonds was crawling in to encircle a fire. A baby squalled. I loped down. They were grim as snakes, stark-faced, bony and ragged, with bleeding feet. The baby nursed and squalled, then tightened his hold on teat, and nursed again. Then squalled, for his haggard Mam was dry.

"Shh," I heard one whisper, "it's only a dog."

But five or six edged off into the trees.

Yes, I told them, for if the watchman sees a fire, you will be chased on out of here.

I looped back up the road, lapped in by Union Street, hung in at dark corner, and took good sighting on Ralph Cawdrey's half-shuttered stall. I heard him over by High Cross giving someone his rent-roller's talk. I zipped in, locked tooth on hind leg of mutton, and staggered off. Hung in at my dark corner. No one. Safe. No cry of "Hang that dog!"

Plopped back up Warwick, slithered on my belly through tall grass to the squaller's Mam. Dropped mutton into the startled creature's lap. Slithered away.

"What was that?" I heard someone say.

"Dog," someone whispered back.

"Mutton!" the little mother peeped.

A whimpering sob or two, hunger's exclamation—and before I was back to town the scent of roasting meat, plume of smoke in the woods, which only another dog would fathom.

One of the Fagan boys, given to passing nasty rumor

and throwing cats into air, stumbled out of the Swan and, without thinking, I bit him. Only knowing I long had been wanting to.

I chawed and clawed at the High Cross pillory, but could do not much with it, so merely lifted my leg and piddled.

I squatted down, grunting my worth, at Cawdrey's door.

For another ten minutes I went truly berserk, racing from one end to the other of the town, barking and snarling and touching tooth to whatever it was that moved.

The Ainge boy went screaming as I spotted him, and clumped down on his face in water as he tried leaping ditch. "Hark to these words, Ainge," I told him. "Leave witch be."

I bayed from the highest knoll, calling out bear. Let bear come, I thundered, him who would scratch Mam.

Calling out Black Shag and his chisely Regarders. Saying: Cut Hooker at your peril, come now and he'll cut thee. But the streets stayed shut up and silent. It stayed hobbled. Night hunkered down. The black sky fermented and rumbled but stayed out of range.

So I trouble-footed it home. Why not? Hooker's time was over. Hooker had had his petty-paced hour.

A dog's trot takes him past smoking chimney and chill, past field, cranny, and nook; it takes him over ground where was laid not-quite-remembered bone, past sodding brook and sodding hill to nuzzle snake's hole and hare's trail and the mole's endless dig; it takes him down narrow ditch and up sweeping slopes and across ghostly divides; it takes him through the curious muck fills; it

takes him the long way, going at it swift-gaited as a
racehorse or moaning low with unfathomable heartsick-
ness—but in the end, tongue dragging, it gets him there.
Blind purpose powers him home.

No, we'd never leave. Crawl up under crow's wing.
Let the hatchetmen come.

Marr greeted me, sniffing close to take the mark of
where I'd been. "I see you bit Ainge," she said. "Have
good pleasure? It's been a sow's dull hour around here."

Henley was closed up tight, which did not astonish,
for in this England Two Foot is up and at chore before
the town's two clocks can strike four.

"You're moody, Mr. Hooker," Marr said.

A rat unblinkered his blinkers and scrambled up the
mud wall.

I trotted over to our clack-dish, the eternal emptiness
of which was the abiding mystery of my life. It was
empty yet, though I licked it all the same. My own
tongue's taste was all that came back to me. Ugg. (Arf.)

"Some chisel man was spying on the house," said
Marr. "Waiting for you. But my growls and the bell-
man's vigilance made him turn in."

A fat slug, eyes in the front of its feet in the odd
way they have, shifted its feelers as I pawed it and its
putrid trail. I nosed it belly-side up, indifferent to my
purpose, my mind at willy-nilly roam through the loose-
dropped night.

"Will he gibbet you, Mr. Hooker? Will they slice
your throat?"

Could a slug stand up? Could a slug grip leaf, hop a
cart, and to London go? Could he script and mouth a

play? I vouchsafe not. Slug is dreamy with his easy life. He drinks his water through at both ends and gets more than enough. What would slug want gold epaulette for, or rapier, or kidskin glove, or civet's wash, or golden tunic that had on it Crest of Slug? Or clack-dish to hold his very own tod of bone meal. Slug stays slug. He stays one piece a dog won't chew.

The moon droned low. A giant's dog-eye looking through history for its other half.

In London I could have baited bears. I could have become Mighty Hooker, best bear-baiter ever. With a little luck I could have made my old Mam proud.

"You're in mood," Marr said again.

I growled her silent. "Kick a dog," I told her. "Go to the fair."

True enough, though: the black cat was sucking my blood.

Rubbish had blowed up over Wolfsleach's death plot. He lay covered in blackness, quiet as a leaf pile. Subdued as a mulching box.

I humbled over. I would have to give him my final heart's leak. My "Go and I go with you" death's preach. Throw up another HERE LIES.

Yea, pitch Hooker and Wolf, two more dead dogs, in.

"What's this?" I said.

For leaf and rubbish is all there was.

"Oh, Wolf's gone," said Marr.

Gone? My flesh wrinkled, my nose glued up. I felt a curious twist of nerves in my tail. My fur stood up. Could the dead walk? Could fallen mange rise?

"Gone?" I said. "You mean the Two Foot moved him?"

Marr laughed. "Not by your wicket," she said. "Wolf got up on his own merit, after the longest sleep ever I saw."

"Wolf's not dead?"

"Why no, Mr. Hooker, whoever said he was! Wolf's gone back to a Snitterfield cove where I think it is he comes from. And Mr. Hooker—I hope you won't be mad—"

"Mad?"

Her news was extraordinary, wrapping knots in my tail. My throat was all chugged up.

"Terry went with him. You know yourself she's come of age now. She said she'd let you know when her whelping comes. Ain't it grand? You'll have nieces and nephews."

I slack-jawed down. My leg thumped dirt. Some magic, I thought. Some plumed sorcerer footloose in the world.

I dabbled off into sleeptime, dreaming of great standing bowls packed with meat. I dreamed of soothy hawks with their breasts ripped open and helpless in my paws, dreamed of grey buzzardry bones choking my throat, dreamed of deer-chasing across new-fallen snow. I pugged onto tough spiny pigs and letched them clean. I bayed at the moon and sniffed worms in the bowels of a dead horse and ate what was good; in my fierce night rule, I chased cluckers off their sitting poles and bit off their heads; I gave the gibbers chase round and around the snake tree; I galloped after cart wheel and coach plug and mammocked a polecat of considerable heft. Beneath a table at the alehouse, I found crusty loaf and chawed on that. In a clear and shallow pool where a bear's bottom had drummeled down, I drank to more good dreams, cooling off my insides with a dog's great fortune. I ate through the entire night of dream, yet my stomach stayed churning; it stayed unfulfilled.

I dreamed of Mam.

I howled over her dead body and came a corpseway's length of licking her.

I saw Terry and Wolf at romp through a twilight dale.

I saw Marr and in my dream contemplated her virtues and defaults. As virtue, she was first and foremost a dog. As default, she was disagreeably harloty. Not clean, not refined, not faithful. Not subtle. She made huge noises eating. She was aloof, a whiner, a foamer. She required frequent grooming. Required a firm hand. She was irascible, irresponsible, a diddler. She was an eye-gouger, a tail-yanker, an ear-puller, a back-sitter, a leg-chewer. A leaner. She lacked any desire to please. She was nervous, opinionated, and largely deaf.

But she was a dog, and I would miss her.

For in my dream I was already past my old life and on the road to Londontown. What loomed was Will, and Will with me, and stretching ahead a mighty bridge, and down from us a grand curving sweep of water thick with sails, and in the misty distance a long wave of hills, and down from the hills tall ranks of buildings stacked one upon the other, with steeple and spire holding fast and firm as far as the eye could descry.

"London," Will uttered. "Where our work is."

And I thought mournfully of the dead fallow deer back at Chalfont Wood, brought down by dog's greed, by beast that had once imagined himself a hunter—of gutted deer that was now companion with the firedrake, the puckle, the sporne, with sylph and satyr and all the witch-world conjurors.

Hooker, I thought, the murderer. Which of us now shall have it hardest?

Will's visage between the antlers, converting me to I knew not what.

And then I came truly awake, to Will's urgent shaking.

"Hurry!" he said. "Here's breakfast. Eat and bid your adieus and let's shake tail out of here before the Regarders come!"

I grumbled up, and there was Marr wagging her tail, and over by the back-door plank was Will hugging Anne, and Susanna and the twins all roped around his neck —with John stepping in to grasp and shake his hand and put money into it and his mother kissing him and weeping and Joan and Gilbert and young Edmund squirt rushing in, and even a neighbor or two, all whispering, "Hurry! Hurry! Before the Regarders come!"—and throwing up their cheer, their fine farewells, saying, "If thou must, William! As the stars script it, William and Hooker! Do it, love! Go, you and Hooker. Go and make us proud!"

And so we went—yea, we went—and did.

A NOTE ON THE AUTHOR

Leon Rooke, a native of North Carolina, now
lives in Victoria, British Columbia. His work has
appeared chiefly in Canada, with the exception
of his novel *Fat Woman* and, now, *Shakespeare's
Dog*. He has been awarded the Canada-Australia
Literary Prize for his achievement in fiction, and
has twice received major fellowships from
the Canada Council of the Arts.

A NOTE ABOUT THE TYPE

This book was set on the Linotype in Fairfield, a type face designed by the distinguished American artist and engraver Rudolph Ruzicka. This type displays the sober and sane qualities of a master craftsman whose talent has long been dedicated to clarity. Rudolph Ruzicka was born in Bohemia in 1883 and came to America in 1894.

This book was composed by Maryland Linotype Composition Co., Baltimore, Maryland. It was printed and bound by The Haddon Craftsmen, Inc., Scranton, Pennsylvania. The typography and binding design were done by Albert Chiang.